TURNER

TURNER

WHITE WOLF RIDGE

C.M. STEELE

C.M. STEELE PRESS

ISBN: 978-1-954645-01-1

CONTENTS

1

Turner

She cries out my name over and over, demanding I make her mine. I'm just about to bite down on her neck....

Ring, ring, ring.

A roar rips through my chest. I close my eyes and try to go back to sleep, but my phone continues to go off. I grumble, seeing the sun shining through my living room windows. I pick up the phone and see it's already after eight.

I shoot her a text, telling her I'll call in twenty. I'm going to be late, but it's my fucking company. It's not like anyone can fire me. I hop in the shower and wash up before putting on a nice clean suit. I'm down my stairs and making a single serving of coffee for my travel mug.

When I'm finally in my Tahoe, I give my assistant a call back to go over shit and get my head on straight before I make it to the resort.

"Hello, Alpha. Did you get a nice sleep?" she asks with some hope in her voice.

"Yes. I did, as it happens, but it seems my to-do list is twice as long today," I grumble, voice laced with sleep.

"Sometimes that's the way it goes. At least you got some sleep so you can just power right through it." I keep her around for these little pep talks.

"What's the point of being in charge when I'm the one doing all the work?"

"Maybe you should learn to delegate. I'm pretty sure that's what bosses do." Yep. Really love her pep talks.

"Keep that snark to yourself, Daphne." She won't.

"I will when you start working smarter. As it is, I'm about to birth these pups soon, so you're going to need to find a replacement," she happily reminds me.

"Ugh. Now why do you have to go and do that? I haven't had my coffee yet, and you're talking about leaving me again. It's not like I have anyone else in mind." It's shitty when you have the perfect assistant and can't find a temporary replacement for her because there isn't anyone capable of taking her place.

"Sorry, but you introduced me to your cousin, and look at where we ended up." I remember exactly how they met. They saw each other when Elijah came over to visit the hotel. When he was younger, he left the pack to go to college and at the same time, Daphne joined our pack with her parents. They were in a different pack, but she wasn't finding a mate, so her parents felt the urge to move elsewhere and they ended up with us. It didn't take long before he gave up his job because I refused to give her up as my assistant. Now they're both working my nerves with this baby nonsense.

"You know I don't like all this baby talk," I remind her.

I manage to steal a sip from my travel mug. It's refreshing. A nice cup of black coffee with a teaspoon of sugar is all I need to get started most days.

"That's because you don't have a mate. If you did, you'd be up her ass, begging to breed her." I snarl, thinking about my dream woman. She's been on my mind for so long that I believe she has to be real.

I hate that she's right. The girl is always right, so I play my trump card. "It's different. I can work while my mate has our babies when that day finally comes. Your mate is busy working as we speak."

"Whatever. How far out are you?" she huffs. I grin, knowing I won.

"Five minutes." I'm on Bluff Road that leads straight up to the resort's main entrance.

"Good. I'll have someone bring up your breakfast since I'm sure you forgot to eat anything, and then we can go over your agenda for the day."

"Fine. Tell them I want extra bacon this morning," I grumble as my stomach does. I'm hungrier than hell. Must be because I didn't eat much at work and passed out last night.

"I will." She hangs up on me, knowing that she's got shit to do. I can always count on her. Three years, and she hasn't let me down yet. I've never met a more organized person. I pull up to my parking spot, turn off the engine, and pop on out, remembering to take my phone with me.

Daphne's there on the stairs, waiting for me. "Good morning, Mr. Turner." When we're in public or if there is at least a chance of being overheard, she calls me "Mr.

Turner." Most of the pack just calls me Turner, but my full name is Josiah Ethan Turner.

"Good morning, Daphne." I smile and slightly bow my head to greet her.

That's when I overhear a human employee mutter to another employee, "I wonder if that baby is his." What the fuck? I know Daphne's keen sense of hearing didn't miss that comment either. What humans don't understand is that as shifters, we mate for life, so they don't understand how a male could be close to a female without trying to fuck her.

I growl, but Daphne puts her hand on my chest. "Calm down. Your eyes." They must be glowing. I really need to get my wolf at bay. We rush over to the elevator bank, pressing the button to my private elevator.

"Inside, now," I growl as it opens. She taps her card, the doors close, and we immediately take off. Once we reach my floor, we quickly walk past the receptionist, Nancy, who constantly smiles and then greets us with a good morning. I grunt hello and then we rush into my office. She hasn't been overly flirtatious with me like some of the women I've met, but she's too sweet, like someone itching to be noticed. There's nowhere more up than the position she has other than Daphne's, and unless my assistant quits, that won't happen.

"He's fired."

"I'll have it taken care of. Are you sure you're okay?" Her brows knit as she looks at me.

"I'm fine," I grunt, hating the pity and worry that I'm getting. I'm the Alpha of the pack. There isn't anything I can't handle, even though my wolf is going full-blown erratic.

"You're anything but fine. You're a mess. Are you too stressed? I'm only teasing about running out on you. I've been training Nancy to handle little things just in case she has to fill in. No one will be as good as me, but hey, we all can't be amazing."

"I suppose you do have a point."

There's a knock at the door, interrupting our conversation. "That must be your breakfast, Nancy wouldn't let anyone get past the front desk." She walks over and opens the door. The sous chef, Mariano, brings my breakfast tray in. "Here you are, Alpha."

"Are you well?" he asks. He's a shifter as well, so he senses the anger rolling off me.

"I am. I just need a moment. Please have a good day." He nods to both of us and departs quickly, hoping to flee my growing ire.

"Take a seat and relax, Daphne. I swear I'm okay. I'm not even sure why I got so bent out of shape."

"Yeah. I could see my mate being that angry, but not you." She makes another great point. My cousin would rip the valet's head off for such a comment.

"Maybe I should have stayed home today." I blow out harshly, running my fingers through my growing hair. I could use a cut, but I don't have time for it. I take a bite of my bacon and moan. "So let's go over everything while I eat. I promise to pay attention." One thing I learned about my assistant is that she hates repeating herself, especially because someone wasn't paying attention the first time.

I can't let this go on; the matter will be dealt with before we go any further. "Hold that thought. Before you get started, I have to make this call." I pick up the receiver on my desk and call the head of Human Resources, Rachael. "Hello, Rachael. I need you to fire that blond fuck that does valet."

"What? Why?"

"Let's just say that he made some disparaging remarks about my assistant and me that he thought we wouldn't hear," I say, clenching my teeth at the end, seething with overwhelming contempt.

"Done. I'll have security take care of it right now. Also, I need to discuss the new hiring list requirements and potential candidates with you. Are we still on for that meeting?" Meeting? Shit.

I look to my assistant and cover the receiver and whisper, "Meeting with HR today?"

She nods. "Yes, two pm."

"Yes. We're still good," I inform Rachael as if I hadn't forgotten about it.

"I don't know what you're going to do without her," she remarks.

"Tell me about it. Do you know how to be an assistant?" I question. She's a great HR manager, even if she's human.

"Nope. Bye." The line clicks. No one likes working for me, but my assistant tolerates me. I put down the receiver and snatch another slice of bacon off my plate. Maybe my mood's off because I'm hangry.

"You better take it easy. We're not immune to heart issues."

"You've got a point, although the old chief was like ninety, though." That's the reason we got stuck with Chief Anderson. Our old chief decided to go up and die on us from a heart attack.

"You have a point there, but we live a lot longer than humans."

"Well, can we get started?"

She rolls her eyes at me, then starts going over my day.

We spend the next hour going over the plans, making subtle changes, and then I dump my tray off with housekeeping before starting my day outside my office. I do a lot of inspections of the individual cabins personally. I don't have time to inspect them all in one day unless it's the off season, which is only about two months, but so far every single one of them has passed the inspection.

I come back to my office only to have my cell go off, and it's my father.

"Max has been arrested for attacking another guy." There's more that he wishes to say, but I sense it's not a public conversation.

"Who would be stupid enough to arrest him?"

"The chief, of course," he snarls.

We both hate that prick, and so does much of the town. His incompetence, laziness, and all-around asshole persona makes him a terrible sheriff. "I have to go down there. I swear I could kill that motherfucker."

"If you don't get rid of that guy soon, he's going to get himself killed."

"I know. He should have never been hired in the first place."

"Tell me about it. I didn't have a say in that shit, or I would have picked one of our own."

By the time I get off the phone with him, I'm furious. I drop my head, shaking it slowly. This is not what I needed to hear today. Fucking stupid-ass kids. I hang up the phone and call Daphne to come into my office. "What's going on?" she asks as she enters and closes the door. I go over the conversation with my father.

"This doesn't help your agitated mood."

"No, it sure doesn't, but I have to go, so take it easy and send me anything you need done. We open in a few days, and you're already close to bursting."

"Thanks, Turner."

I run out of my office, past my receptionist and to the elevators. It takes only a minute to get down to the lobby, but I'm anxious and pissed off. I'm barely in my truck when my father calls again.

"What's going on?"

"I got your brother out. Meet me at the house, please."

"Okay. I'm on my way now," I snarl, ending the call and speeding off toward my parents' home. I need details about what happened and why he was arrested in the first place. Chief Anderson's pressing my buttons. He doesn't know that he's crossing a dangerous line, but he'll learn the hard way.

As soon as I arrive, my sister's sitting on the sofa with my brother, and my parents are on the loveseat while my mother holds my father's hand.

"Would anyone care to elaborate for me?" I demand.

Aria sighs and then starts to speak. "Timmy came up to me and was harassing me as usual, then this guy I don't know approached and told Timmy to back off and that I was his, so he kissed me, and then knucklehead over here overreacted and clocked the guy just as the chief walked by."

"Who's the bastard that kissed you?"

"He's a shifter from the Wolfe Creek pack."

"Son of a bitch."

"It was just on the cheek. Max is being ridiculous. All of you are being ridiculous. It was nothing but someone protecting me from that damn grabby human asshole."

"I'll deal with Timmy later, but I want to talk to the Wolfe Creek pack leader. I need a word with their people." I send a text to my Beta, Mark. *Set up a meeting with the Wolfe Creek Alpha for the day after tomorrow.* I look up at my family, feeling their nervousness swimming around the room. "I'm not going to let this go."

"Come on. It's stupid," Aria argues.

"Stupid?" I question, and she cowers, sensing my anger as the Alpha. I feel bad immediately because she's my little sister and she's young, but I will not have my will overruled. Sitting next to her, I say, "I just want to talk. I don't want them coming after us." She nods in acceptance.

Leaning over, I punch my brother lightly in the shoulder. "Now how did you get out?"

"I'm the mayor. Who's going to argue with no one pressing any charges? Although that asshole chief wasn't too happy about it."

"He can go fuck himself. Now, if you'll excuse me, I need to get home and get some fucking sleep."

I should let this go. In my head I know it's not worth a

war, but I can't stop the words from coming out of my mouth. As the Alpha, I have to show strength when another pack starts shit with us.

Are they trying to fuck up my multi-billion-dollar business? Wolfe Creek isn't the only vacation resort in the area. Mine runs like a well-oiled machine, and I refuse to let anyone throw a wrench into my perfectly operated business. Unlike their pack, we have a lot of humans running around in all capacities. Some regrettably so, like the chief, so we've learned over the years to tame our inner wolf unless it's a full moon, but that doesn't mean I won't do everything to protect my family.

I say my goodbyes because I'm tired as hell and make my way home. As soon as I'm in the house, I hurry up to my bathroom to shower. Washing my weary bones, I close my eyes and think of my nightly visitor, my temptress, my doom and glory. Each image is vivid, wild, intense, and stars just one delectable creature.

In my most recent dream of her, she's in a police uniform with her hands on her hips. I don't know if she's really a cop, or if it's Halloween. I think about the time of year and do the math. Halloween's eleven months, two weeks away. There's no way I can wait that long. My heart pounds in my chest as I think about her beauty. Long black hair in a ponytail in the middle of her head, smooth and not a hair out of place, at least not until I get ahold of her.

The sound of my phone ringing stops my fantasies of this mysterious woman. I left the fucker in my truck. "Damn it." I wrap a towel around my waist and dash out to my truck. I'm not worried about being seen because I live off a very remote road, but just in case, I make sure to cover up. When I pull the phone out, I see the missed call from Mark. I call him back as I hustle back into the house.

"What's going on?" I snarl into the phone.

"I've heard from their pack leader. They want to meet tomorrow." That's good, but not going to work for me.

"I'm busy. It will have to wait for the day after." I'm not going to let them push me around. I'm the one with an ax to grind.

"Sure thing. I'll set it up."

"Good. Goodnight. I have to be at the main resort at six tomorrow."

Once I slip on a pair of boxers, I dig in the fridge for a snack because I won't be able to sleep with my stomach growling. I really need to make sure I eat more than once a day. I'm six two, two-twenty, and I need more to keep my muscles strong and in peak condition. I eat a bowl of cereal. It's not what I need, but at least it's something. While I do that, I shoot a text to my father to let him know it's on with the other pack.

Like I expected, my phone rings. "Hey, Dad."

"So you're set to meet with them?"

"I am. I want shit straightened out. I don't want trouble for no damn reason, and I'm sure they'll understand our actions, although a bit much, were done to protect our own."

"Just be careful, my son. I don't trust them. They have a lot of tension going on between them, and I'd hate for them to attack you."

"I don't think they want a fight." I'm not sure of that, but I have to go.

"Fine. Trust your gut."

"My gut is telling me to get there as soon as possible to deal with this."

"Sorry, I'm a father. I worry because I love you, son. You've taken over the pack so well that no one even noticed the transition of power."

"Thanks, but I suppose they knew you were grooming me for a long time and that your training had gone off without a hitch. How are you handling not being the Alpha anymore?"

"I'm great. As much as I loved it, I love the freedom of just worrying about my family. I'm still the mayor, which means I play a part in leadership, but I get to pass the burden of keeping the pack in line to you."

"It's easy. They're all doing well, or at least close to well. Most of the unmated members are the ones who are less content. Speaking of content, I'm worried about Max."

"I sense a change in him as well."

"He's restless." I sigh. I'm worried about my brother.

"Maybe he needs a change. He's barely eighteen and learning his place in life. This is why male wolves take longer before reaching their mating age."

"I didn't have that issue."

"No, but that is because you're the heir. Your path has been laid out since the moment you were born. Your footing has been steady. Now, when you have a mate, things might change."

"What do you mean?"

"Well, your behavior may become more erratic, irrational as you do all you can to protect your family."

"You weren't—aren't—like that with us."

"It will settle as time passes. You don't love your mate or your family any less, but the danger feels less striking and around every corner."

"I guess that's good to know."

"It is. Now get some sleep. I've kept you up long enough. I love you, son."

"I love you too," I say, ending the call.

I check the clock on the microwave. Shit. It's just after midnight.

I climb up the stairs and then my head finally hits the pillow. The cool feel of the material immediately sends me to sleep.

Her eyes—chocolate and sweet—focus on me with such wonder that I fear she'll be afraid of the truth, but then they switch to pain and then anger. She's thrashing against me, but I'm not sure why and I sense I'm losing her. "No. You can't leave me," I cry out, and my world goes black.

Waking up in a cold sweat with beads of perspiration dripping down my face and back, soaking my sheets, I toss the covers off, wondering when I actually pulled them on. Hopping off the bed, I pace back and forth, hating and loving the nightly dreams. Who can she be, and why am I dreaming of her? Is she my mate? She must be, but why the premonitions? I don't have them for anything else; I would have known some dumb young pup was going to make a move on my sister and that Max would try to kill him. Instead, I'm left to get the information afterward.

"What the hell is happening to me?" It's not like I can ask anyone. I don't have friends close enough who have experienced anything like this. Even my pack members, Beta included, would think I was nuts to be having these dreams, passionate, vivid fantasies filled with hot, sweaty sex and multiple orgasms.

Thrusting my hands into my short, dark brown hair, I tug on the wet strands, hoping to pull myself out of this endless torture.

I need a run. I step out into the icy night air in just my boxers, shucking them off, and dash through the trees, shifting as soon as the forest gives me cover. The shift is seamless; years of transforming has created nothing more than a blur as if it's just your imagination that I was anything other than a wolf when my white paws land on the freshly fallen blanket of snow. I close my eyes and breathe in the cold, loving the smell washing off the trees. Nothing but fresh pine as winter arrives early. The hooting of a nearby owl reminds me of my mission to shake off enough energy to fall asleep.

Beautiful, I'll find you and once I do, there will be nothing to stop me from making my dreams a reality. I howl and sprint, racing through an open pass and then back into a thick forest up the side of the mountain. It's perfect for this week, I think. The snow's ready for skiing, or at least it will be in two days or so. I feel it under my paws and itch to get on my board. It's one hell of a benefit of being a winter creature. I live for these days. I hope my mate will feel the same way.

I run for miles, ending up on the other side of the ridge, looking over to the town that holds my empire.

Will I have a mate to continue that future? That thought brings me back to the vision in my dreams. The whole purpose was to shake her from my mind so that I can get a peaceful sleep. I run harder and faster, racing back to the house until I'm practically panting. I finally make it to my porch and pick up my boxers with my teeth before nudging the door open with my nose.

I smell the air, making sure I'm alone, and then I shift. No one should be in my home, but you can never be too sure with hikers who get lost and seek shelter. It's happened only once, and thankfully I'd been out working and came home in my human form to a couple on my porch, cuddling up on the blanket on my bench. I gave them something warm to drink, let them sit by the fire, and then drove them back into town. Since then, I've been a little more careful, installing security. It doesn't go off when I'm coming and going because it has both my human and wolf form saved, but it does for everyone else.

2

Maria

I WAKE up from a cold sweat, my body tingling in ways that are hard for me to explain. It's as if I'm being devoured by ecstasy and freed by pleasure. Every morning I wake up the same way: flushed, sweaty, feeling exhausted and craving more of *him* and those eyes. I feel like I've seen eyes like that before, but I haven't. Many of the men in this town have similar eyes. Bright, determined, shining with something different, but they aren't his—my nightly dream lover.

I whip the covers off me and swing my feet onto the cold floor of my bedroom, feeling stupid. *Eyes.* Seriously, I'm losing it. I think this town is getting to me. Everything is too damn mysterious and cliquey.

The Wolfe family seem to rule everything, and even the sheriff, Erik Smith, follows their lead. It's not that I don't like the Wolfes, but they give me a supernatural feeling that makes me think I've gone completely insane.

There's no way that things like that exist, but I feel like I've stepped into some film with a bunch of large, handsome men with a lot of secrets and a love of growling. I think the wilderness has gotten to most of them. Maybe that's what happens when you end up where people live around the woods like the animals.

I'm off today after a long day yesterday of patrolling the Wolfe Creek area. Most days there's not much to do, but randomly there's a fight or two between teenagers or guests at the hotel who have had too much to drink, or not enough. There hasn't been much trouble in the past few years since I started here, but there were a few incidents that took me by surprise, like the shooting of the sheriff. Erik miraculously survived being shot in the head, which made me wonder more about the whole superhuman thing. I'm not sure why, exactly, I am convinced there's something strange going on. Maybe it's all the television shows and movies that have me on edge.

Still, if I'm honest with myself, it has more to do with my dreams than anything else. For nearly six months, I've felt the pull to the same man. He's more than a man. It's written in his eyes and in his build. He's not as large as Hunter or Erik, but he's not small either. He's around six foot two, which still towers over my whole five two stature. Every night he visits me in my sleep, kissing and worshipping me until we're both too exhausted to continue.

My entire life, I never expected to need a man, but this man, whoever he is, has created a hole that I know only he can fill.

I like working for Erik, but I can't stand the nagging

feeling that I'm being left out. My entire life I've been left out, mostly because of my size and sex, which only made me more determined to prove them all wrong. Although I'm not sure who I'm still trying to prove anything to; everyone around here actually respects me. I hadn't gotten that reception initially, but then Mr. Wolfe put his foot down and everyone seemed to just go by his word. He appeared to have more pull than the sheriff himself.

The front door slams open, and my roommate, Jacob, enters. "Oh my God. What the hell happened to you?"

"Nothing. I got into a fight. I'm fine. I thought you would be at work right now," he barks out at me. I know this is only because he got beat up, and when someone tough gets hurt, they take it out on others. He needs to chill out, though, or I'll add to the bruising. I'm only trying to be nice.

He says it with an accusatory tone that pisses me off. I took the guy in when he needed a place to live. "No. I'm not. Today's my day off."

A knock follows, and in comes Hunter with Erik behind him. "Crabtree. We need to have a word with you in private," Hunter orders.

"Maria, please excuse us." They walk right past me and into Jacob's room. Whispers start, and I can't hear anything. How the fuck can they even hear each other?

Since they don't care to share, I go into my room and get changed so I'm not just in my pajamas in front of my boss. Fuck it. I'm living with a young man because they said it was the best place for both of us, and it has been. Jacob's a good man, so it pisses me off that he's injured, but if he doesn't want to tell me what happened, then there's nothing I can do.

I come out after a shower and get dressed, and then Hunter and Erik walk out into the living room. "How's Jacob? What happened?"

"He's going to be fine. Boys fighting over girls kind of thing."

"Okay. How's the other guy?" I question. Obviously, this must have been some serious issue. I've never seen Jacob act that way with females. He doesn't even seem to notice them.

"Same."

"Well, I hope it's over with."

"It better be," Hunter snarls. I'm taken aback by his tone as he looks towards Jacob's room as if he's the supreme authority in Jacob's life. He grabs the door, yanking it open, and leaves with Erik following behind without another word. I sigh as I lock the door behind them and walk into the kitchen to get a drink, only to be caught off guard by Jacob sitting at the table.

"Are you okay?" I'm worried about him. He's become a little brother to me, and I'd hate to see anything happen to him.

"I'm going to be fine. It's nothing. Please try not to worry about me. I swear it's nothing."

"I didn't even know there was a girl you liked," I say.

"Well, it doesn't matter because I don't plan to see her for a long time." He runs his hand through his slicked-back black hair.

"Why were they here? To take a report of the incident?

Where did it happen?" As a police officer, I can't help but ask questions.

"It happened out of town. They were just worried about me because the girl's father is the mayor."

"What were you doing out of town?" He never mentioned leaving, even for a short trip. Not that he has to say shit, but it would be considerate since he always keeps tabs on me.

"No offense, Maria, but I've had enough questions for the day. I just want to go to sleep," he says.

"I understand. Take some meds and go to bed." He nods and walks out of the kitchen. I'm sure he's exhausted. He's been patched up, so he sought medical treatment somewhere. Ugh, I feel helpless, and it's not something I care for.

I make some coffee and attempt to get over someone else's problems. I should go and talk to Erik and see if there's anything I can do to smooth things over, maybe talk to this little viper of a girl who thinks she can turn Jacob's world upside down and leave him broken.

I'm in the middle of my first cup of coffee when I get a call from Erik. "Hey, Doug just called in sick. Can you cover for him?"

"Sure, but you know that's going to put me at time and a half, right?" I remind him.

"That's fine. Thanks to the added revenue in town, we can afford it. See you at the station in an hour?"

"Sure." I guess today's not my day off.

"Jacob, I have to go in. Do you need anything?"

"No. Thanks. Have a safe day, Maria," he mumbles. The brush-off isn't what I expected, but given the events of the past hour, I suppose that's all the send-off I'm going to get.

I'm ready to go in ten minutes since I've already showered. I go out and drive to the station in my new Chevy Silverado. It's the first time I get to have my own nice new vehicle, and I love it. It drives well in this area and it's perfect for any snowfall we may get. It's all black and has all the fancy tech I've never had before. I turn on the music, listening to the Beatles Station on XM because I've got an old soul. I barely get through *Can't Buy Me Love* when I'm already at the police station. Boo. It makes me want to take a road trip, maybe visit some family down south. I do have a vacation coming in two months. Perhaps I can go to Texas and see my parents. It'll be close to Christmas time then. I'm the only one in my family who hates the heat. They don't mind burning up, wrinkling faster in the Texas heat.

"Good morning," I say, entering the station.

"Wow, we're surprised to see you back so soon," Darren says, taking a bite out of a donut from the bakery down the street.

"Yeah, well, you know I've got nothing else to do in this town."

"We need to find you a man." Normally, I'd just ignore that, but in the back of my head, I feel like even talking about dating makes me feel uneasy. As if I'm betraying my nightly visitor. It makes no damn sense.

"Maybe I will." I have a body that has all the right curves despite my athletic yet short physique, and I have a pretty face, or so I'm told. I don't wear a lot of makeup, but I'm not the stereotypical, overly unfeminine female cop. I've got a lot to prove, but that doesn't mean I don't like looking like a girl. My hair's a mix of curly and straight, but some days, I straighten it or I let it go all natural. Since I didn't have time to prepare, my hair is pinned up in a tight ponytail, but it will get fluffy as it dries. Genetics.

"That's what I like to hear," Gretchen, the dispatcher, says.

"So where am I supposed to meet men?"

"I'm not sure, but maybe you should stop by the resort one of these days, and there will be a lodge full of men who can't take their eyes off you. You are pretty damn hot," Tony says. He's been here as long as I have, and we both work patrol most days.

"He's got a point. You could probably have any single guy that caught your eye," Gretchen adds while filing her nails. I'm not even sure why they need me here. There isn't much to do even with the growth of the town. It's still pretty calm most days. It's the nights that get a little unruly, but even so, I don't take night shifts. Erik is extremely clear on that.

As the only female patrol officer on the force, he doesn't want me to be alone. A lot of people are tourists, and so something could happen to me and no one would know who did it. He has a point. I dared him once, and he had me go to the mat with some of the larger men at the station. I held my own for a minute, but I'd always been taken down in the end. I might be a tough cookie, but not when going up against a brick wall. I learned my lesson and held off asking to patrol at night.

"Well, it hasn't happened yet. I won't hold my breath.

So is there anything that needs dealing with, or am I just going on a cruise?"

"They could use someone to handle traffic up at the exit off the interstate. There are a lot of travelers headed this way, and it's chaotic. I'm taking the next two hours. I don't know if you'll be my replacement."

"Okay. Let me know if you need me," I say. Tony nods and walks out of the station, stealing a donut from the box on the counter. He's a good guy, works hard, and never misses a shift.

"So the boss man called you in with nothing to do. Come over here and let me do your nails while we have time to kill." I try to dissuade her, but honestly I could use a little pampering.

"I'd usually say no, but I need a spa day."

"Yes. How about we go after work? We only have to be here until four. The salon at the resort is open to eight. I'll book us for five."

"That sounds so good." I could really use it. I sigh.

Just then, someone calls. There's a car accident, and I'm needed. I jump up and grab my keys to the patrol car and head out to take the report.

"*A*h, this is just what I needed," I say, relaxing in the middle of my massage. Slowly I start to fall asleep, and then my dream guy pops into my head. I flip out and jolt awake.

"Whoa! Are you okay?"

"Yes. Sorry, I guess I didn't realize I'd fallen asleep."

"Who is Turner?" the masseuse asks.

"What do you mean?" I ask, lifting my head off the table and tilting it slightly to see her.

"You called out his name. I don't know anyone around here with that name. Could it be from where you lived before?"

"No. I don't know a Turner." Then it surprises me that it's the first time I've made it out of my dream with his name. I guess there has never been anyone to hear me say it, and I've never remembered it before. *Turner*, I repeat to myself, loving the way it rolls off my tongue.

"Well, maybe you were just dreaming about turning over or something. I could have heard you wrong." Maybe, or that's really his name. I'm betting it's the latter. Goodness, my pulse picks up and I wonder what else I said in my sleep.

"Thanks. Am I done now?" I ask, feeling incredibly relaxed.

"Yes, your nails are next on your list for the day. You can cover back up in your robe and take this hallway down and then to the left."

"Thank you." I wrap up in the nice fluffy robe after she leaves the room. I've never had this type of luxury. I feel spoiled, but this is not going to be a common occurrence because I can't afford it on my salary. Still, a girl could use this treatment every six months at least.

By the end of a relaxing day, I run into the owner of the hotel and his lovely wife, Hunter and Catherine Wolfe. "Hello, Deputy Arroyo."

"Hello. I have to say your spa is magnificent," I gush over the fabulous treatment.

"Thank you. I hope you enjoyed it. I spent months improving it based on Cat's suggestions," Hunter says, seeming less angry than before.

"Us women know what women want," she says with a conspiratorial wink.

"Have a good night." I walk out and hand my ticket to the valet. My truck is brought around within a minute, and then I'm off to relax.

When I get to the apartment, Jacob's in his room. "Welcome home, Maria." This time he's more cheerful, but he doesn't bother to come out of his room, which is fine by me.

"Thank you. Goodnight. I have a five am start. See you tomorrow night."

"Goodnight." I like that he's more chipper than he sounded this morning.

Stripping down to my panties, I grab my nightgown and slip it on. Sleep easily takes over because I'm so relaxed. The second my eyes close, I'm out like a light.

By three in the morning, I'm up and getting ready for another day on the job, but I look and see a note from Jacob. *I had to go out. I'll be back tomorrow night. Don't worry about me.*

"What?" I call his cell, but it goes straight to voicemail.

Damn it. I make coffee and get ready for work, all the while thinking about Jacob and where he had to go in the middle of the night. It doesn't make sense. Everything about him has been different the past few days. It makes me nervous.

I work the whole day, thinking about Jacob. He hasn't

answered his phone or even returned my calls and texts. Erik's supposed to be at the station all day, but I only see the sheriff once. I try to talk to him, but he does his best to act busy. Then he has to leave just as I'm getting off work. I don't like it, so I follow him and he's at Hunter's home. I wait, and then I see another vehicle pull up. It takes me a few minutes to work up the nerve to interrupt whatever's going on. I'm barely out of my car when Hunter and Erik come out, scowling. Then, before I know it, someone pushes from behind them. My mouth drops open, and my legs feel like they're about to buckle.

3

Turner

MARK and I make the trip to Wolfe Creek, even though I'd prefer that he stayed back in White Wolf, but he's hard of hearing and insisted I not go alone. Within a few minutes on the road, he's already testing my patience.

"I should have left your ass back there," I say, giving him a deathly glare.

"Nah. You're already on edge. Your wolf has been ready to strike, and don't lie to me either. You're raging, and it doesn't even make sense. Your father—hell, even you have said that your brother overreacted, and we're the ones who should make amends."

"I know, but that doesn't mean I'm not supposed to show a strong, united front. He touched my sister, and that automatically put him in my crosshairs. I just want their word that we don't have a problem."

"And a phone call wasn't sufficient?"

"Obviously fucking not. If it was, I wouldn't be going.

Now, are you going to drive and stop being a whiny bitch?" I hiss, itching to slam his head on the steering wheel.

"Damn, as long as you don't act that way with Hunter Wolfe, we'll be good." He reaches over and turns on the radio. The Beatles are on, and for the first time I don't hate it. I let it play and then attempt to relax, which strangely happens. It's early afternoon, but it gets dark early at this time of year and although I trust them not to act up, being in another's territory after dark isn't smart.

"We're about twenty minutes out from his property. He's supposed to just have his Beta with him, so if he's honest, then we've got nothing to worry about." The snow turns to rain as we get closer to their place, but then stops altogether and the sun suddenly comes out. It's strange, but my wolf feels restless.

We're about a quarter mile from his home when my wolf growls and I look out the window. It looks like there's a vehicle out there, but we're moving too fast to check it. Oddly, I don't sense a foreboding and danger. I swear for a minute I feel my dick jerk. That can't be right, unless Hunter lied about having someone else being there. Although, if it is her, then I don't care if he lied to me.

"We're here," Mark says, pulling into a long driveway. "Okay, Alpha. You let me know what you need me to do. I've got your back, as always."

"I will. Just keep your cool. I have a good feeling about this," I say, sensing my wolf is excitable. *She's near.* We exit the vehicle cautiously and then make our way to the porch. I'm greeted by two large men, who make introductions. Hunter Wolfe and his Beta.

"What's with the gun?" Mark says, eyeing the holster on the Beta.

"I'm the sheriff. I'm always carrying." He doesn't flinch and stands strong, which is good for both parties.

"Hey, don't get bent out of shape. I just asked. We want this to be peaceful as possible," he says, tossing his hands up in surrender.

Wanting to get this over with, Hunter gets right to the point. "Okay, so two of our young ones got into a fight, but what I don't understand is why."

I thought they would have talked to the kid. "It's because I told my younger brother to protect my little sister. She's a teen, and well, I don't want any men sniffing around her. She's not mating age yet, so when the Crabtree kid kissed her, my brother was on him."

"Let me ask you something. Did you ever think that they'll mate once she's of age?" the sheriff asks me, which raises my hackles. Is he itching for a fight?

I snarl out, "Even if it was possible, why is he kissing her now?"

"Why would you care? He can't fuck her," Hunter asks.

"I didn't react. My little brother did. But it still doesn't excuse what he did," I say, defending our actions.

"He said it was because some human boy was flirting with her, and he didn't appreciate it. Erik, why don't you go ahead and tell them about how you met my sister?" Hunter asks his second.

The sheriff chuckles, but I see the pain behind his

eyes. He's married to the Alpha's sister, which means Hunter understands about having a little sister too. "He probably kissed her because he's young and his mating starts next year. If he feels anything like what I felt for my mate before I mated with her, then his heart is hurting. Jealousy eats at him constantly. It can leave you empty and sad, craving for her just to be near. Have you met your mate yet?"

A low growl rips through my chest painfully, as if the lonely ache has tripled from just the mention of a mate. I need to find my mate. The wolf within me grows increasingly agitated.

Hunter looks at me sympathetically. "So you have, but you're not mated yet. How long has it been?"

He understands what I'm going through? "Five months, three weeks, two days, and twelve hours," I say with another soul-aching growl.

Erik chimes in. "I fell in love with Chloe a year before our full mating kicked in. Our mating instinct waited until I was worthy of her and became the Beta. I spent a year in purgatory—looking, wishing, and hoping I could touch her. I don't know how many times I almost kissed her or how many times I snarled at another man for speaking to her. If I'd been younger, I don't think I'd have the self-control to stop myself. When I thought all was hopeless, the change happened."

"A year?" My pulse picks up and my chest burns at that information. I can't wait a year. I'll go insane.

"A year," the sheriff repeats. "The longest year of my life."

"So she's his mate?" Mark asks about the punk and my sister.

Erik and Hunter shrug and then Erik says, "More than likely, and until the time is right, they're both going to be suffering. The best thing to do would be limit their contact with the opposite sex, but don't keep them from each other. Jealousy only heightens the need to claim what they can't. Keeping them apart will make it worse." I make a mental note regarding their suggestion, although I'll see for myself in due time.

"Thanks," I say, shaking Erik's hand, and when I'm about to shake Hunter's, I hear the sound of tires crunching gravel.

"I thought you said it was just the two of you," I snarl. My wolf's curious about who just arrived.

Hunter's brows bunch together in aggravation. "It is. If it's my wife, I'm going to spank her ass." Whoever's here isn't supposed to be. Hunter has a scowl etched on his face as he marches to the front of the house.

"Mine too," Erik says, walking behind him.

We all take a whiff of the air, but I know it's not their mates because the smell is different, and I know it. It haunts me during my waking hours. It's burned into my soul, etched on my heart, embedded in me. It's *her*. I run right past them and straight to her. "It's you!" I say as I rush to stand in front of a petite officer with chocolate eyes and perfect everything.

"It's you!" she shouts out. Unable to stop myself, I drag her into my arms, lacing my fingers through her ponytail and slamming my lips onto hers. A wave of lust slams through me, demanding I take more.

"Wow, didn't see that coming," Hunter remarks. I barely make out the words because I can't get enough of her. She clings to me with her legs around my waist, knowing we're one. I'm a wild man, a beast ready to claim his other half.

I hear their footsteps through my mating haze and snarl, turning to them while holding her to me protectively. They wave me off like I've lost my damn mind, which is pretty accurate. I know that more than anything, she's taken all my rhyme or reason.

"Turner, you two are more than welcome to go to the resort. I'll call and make the reservation for the next two days," Hunter says, pulling his phone out of his pocket.

"Thanks," I say, and then I turn to my mate because she deserves my attention. "Let's go."

"Have fun, and don't do anything I wouldn't."

I flip Hunter off and then flip my mate over my shoulder, carrying her to my SUV without waiting for approval from anyone, including my mate. I don't care that she came in a squad car or that she's probably on duty.

"Hey, what about me?" Mark says.

I stop, turning my head slowly and glaring at my Beta. "Walk," I growl before helping her into the passenger seat.

"Whoa. Where are you taking me? Who are you?" she exclaims, pumping the brakes on the situation.

"I'm your mate. Can't you feel it?" I question, sensing a bit of resistance.

"I don't know what you're talking about," she says. I can feel her lust rolling off her, but for the first time, my brain processes what I instinctively knew the second she pulled up—she's human.

"Shit," I growl, closing the door and sprinting around to the other side of the SUV to hop in. I'm pulling out of the driveway before she has a chance to object.

"Forgive me. I'll slow this down," I say, nearly choking on my words as if they're forced violently from my throat. "I'm Josiah Turner. I'm from White Wolf Ridge." It's all I can manage to vocalize at the moment.

"I'm Deputy Maria Arroyo." Her eyes stare into mine as she nibbles on her bottom lip and then swipes her tongue along the edge. "What do you mean by 'mate'?" she asks, wringing her fingers nervously while tearing her eyes away from me and onto the road around us.

"Calm yourself, love. I won't hurt you. I could never, ever hurt you." I attempt to reassure her, but I'm not sure she's on board with the suddenness of the situation.

"I don't understand why..." she waves her hands between us "...this connection. I don't understand it."

"I don't know everything, but I believe Hunter Wolfe knows exactly what's going on."

"Why does everyone run everything past Hunter? Besides him being a know-it-all." Damn, she doesn't seem to like him, which makes me feel better, but then a sense of dread fills me. She has no idea what we are and what we mean to each other now.

"You don't really know the truth." I pull off to the side of the road.

"What are you doing?" Her tension elevates a notch or two, but it's not from fear. Desire pools between her thighs and invades my nostrils. I want to strip her bare and taste her, let her scent envelop me.

"We need to talk, and I can't leave you feeling so upset."

"We can talk at the hotel," she argues.

"I'm afraid we cannot. I won't be able to control this raging longing once we are left alone without interruption."

"We're alone here." She takes a deep breath, and I know her body's begging for mine. I reach up and brush her cheek with the back of my fingers.

"Anyone can pass by," I remind her. It's that notion that staves off my hunger long enough to pull my thoughts together. "Maria," I say, pausing, trying to figure out how to say this. "Listen. Hunter, your sheriff, and me. We're not just human."

"Oh my God. What are you?"

"We're wolf shifters." Her face whitens and then she laughs, shaking her head.

"That's nuts."

"Then how come you jumped into my arms as if you've known me? Let me rub my scent all over you?" She's about to say something smart, so I put my fingers to her lips. "Trust me, mate. Do not say something like 'I do that all the time' because I'll tear this town apart, killing every single man here who thinks you are theirs. You belong to me." I sound possessive, and I am. My father had been right. The second I found my mate, the world would flip on its head and I'd become more irrational than a motherfucker.

"There's no one else, but I don't understand this. You can't be real."

"I could say the same for you. For nearly six months I dreamed of you, and yet here you are as if I'm still dreaming."

"You too?" A dawning strikes her.

"See? I've never heard of it before, but something Hunter said told me he understood my plight more than your sheriff did."

"Oh my goodness, how many are there of you?"

"There's only one of *me*, but there are thousands of shifters throughout the world."

"Wow. I don't even know what the hell is going on."

"Why were you there in the first place?" I growl. It's been on my mind because if she wasn't there for me, then why would she be at the home of another Alpha? Jealousy fills my soul like a mad beast.

"Your eyes just flashed a brighter blue," she says.

"My mate, please explain." I take a deep breath, attempting to control the urge to mate with her right here. I need to mark her so everyone knows she's mine.

"My roommate disappeared today, and I was looking for him." I stop her right there and undo her belt, lifting her onto my lap.

"You're mine and you've been living with another man?" I snarl, cupping the back of her head.

"You don't own me." Fuck. Please don't do this. I feel the bond cracking. I can't let that happen. I need my queen to rule by my side. She attempts to break my hold, which is futile.

"Maria. Damn it. You own me more than you can ever,

ever, ever imagine. I live for you, now and until the end of my days. We're fated to be together. I wish I could even explain what you mean to me."

She reaches up and touches my face. "Don't be upset, Turner. I'm scared, but for some reason, I trust you more than I can even comprehend. It's as if you mean more to me than is even rational. I just need time to absorb what this all means. I've been living around these people and completely unaware."

"I can't tell you anything about them because I don't know much about them, other than Hunter, because he's the Alpha of this pack. He's the one I came to talk to about some trouble his people made in my area two days ago."

She freezes. "Is this about Jacob?"

"Who the fuck is this Jacob?" Just hearing her speak another man's name with such concern pokes at my green monster.

"My roommate. The one who has gone missing."

"He better not be in White Wolf again," I mutter to myself with a little more tension than I should. I'm supposed to be relaxing her, not scaring her.

She's not scared, though. She's glaring at me with such appalling anger. "So you did that to him?"

Normally I wouldn't even dare to explain myself, but she is my mate. "No, and before you ask, I don't know where he's at."

She's about to ask more questions—I can see it in her eyes—but I have to make a call.

"Hold on." I say, "Call Max." My SUV rings while we wait for my brother to pick up.

"What's up, Alpha?" he answers on the last ring.

"Be on the lookout for that fuck. Don't hurt him, but keep an eye on his movements should he enter our territory."

"What's going on? Are those fucks giving you shit? I'll be down there."

"No. I don't have beef with the Wolfe Creek pack."

"Okay. So I'll keep Aria safe and not let that fuck bother her. What's his problem?"

"They think he might be her mate, but I don't hold much stock in that shit. I need you to do me a favor. Hold down the fort. I'll be a couple of days. I might send Mark back, but I'm going to be down here for a bit." I know the questions are coming, and I don't even get a chance to answer because he's tossing them out.

"What's going on? You never take a vacation, and the season starts soon. They're going to need you here. Daphne's going to freak out. You can't do that; she's about to have a baby."

"Daphne? You're having a baby with someone? I'm not going to be your other woman," Maria gasps and hollers.

"Whoa. You have your mate. Sorry, brother. I will handle everything." He ends the call abruptly, which is good because I could strangle him. I grab Maria's ponytail a little rougher than necessary and slightly tug her back because she's banging on my chest and is going to hurt herself.

"Calm your sexy ass down. Daphne's my assistant, and our resort opens in a couple of days. She's extremely busy and meticulous, so he's worried about her. Besides, her mate is my cousin."

"Cousin?" she asks, her cheeks heating up with embarrassment.

"Yes, and by the way, love, we only ever have one mate."

"At a time?" She cocks her expertly sculpted brows at me.

"No—one, period. We only get one. You're the only one who does this to me." I groan as I grind my cock against her wet heat. I ache to come right now, but I need to be inside her. We must get to the hotel now. She moans, pulling at my inner beast, teasing the fucker until he's ready to pin her to the backseat and drill into her over and over.

"Enough. We can talk later. I'm barely hanging on to my sanity. I don't think my wolf can handle any more of this." I lift her off me and sit her back into her seat. "Buckle up."

She does, her eyes as hungry as mine. We need to get in before I lose my mind. We're pulling up to the valet, and I'm nearly out of my seat before the vehicle is in park.

"Deputy Arroyo, you're back." I want to break his jaw for even knowing my mate.

"Hunter has a room here for us," I growl at him.

"Please check-in inside. I'll park it." He walks around and gives her a smirk and shakes his head.

"You were here with someone else?" I get the faintest hints of scent on her, but they're fleeting, not embedded in her, but those who pass her or even hug her. I growl, trying to understand that she's human and they don't live by our standards of celibacy. She can go on and live happily with another man while I suffer for the rest of my life.

A woman approaches us with a smile before we're two feet into the lobby. "Hello, Maria." She smiles widely at my mate. She then looks at me with an arched brow. I breath in and know immediately that she's Hunter's mate. "You must be Turner. My husband said to take this to room four hundred four."

"Thank you, Mrs. Wolfe," I say, letting her know without explanation that I know who she is.

"Please, call me Cat, and if you need anyone to speak with, don't hesitate." She pulls Maria in for a hug and whispers, "Welcome to your new world." Of course I can hear her, but that's so the rest of people around don't hear.

"She was human," I whisper as we part ways. "She's Hunter's mate. I smell him on her."

"What? You know that?"

"Yes, and it's probably why she offered to tell you about things. She would know more than others. I have questions for Hunter as well, but they must wait until I have you under me, becoming mine for life."

"I don't understand this, but I don't want to fight it. Cat is one of the most worshipped women in town."

"As you will be in our town. I am the Alpha of the White Wolf Ridge pack, and you're my mate."

"Oh my. Why is that turning me on when you call me your mate?"

"Because your body knows what your mind is denying. It knows you belong to me like I belong to you, and that only by being together are we whole."

"I need you to show me, Turner."

"We'll show each other, my sweet Maria. God, you are a gift I could have never imagined was real." We arrive at the elevators, and I feel like it takes an eternity for one to open. As soon as we enter the empty car, I pin her to the wall and slam my mouth onto hers. She slips her tongue out and I suck it in, letting it tease mine as my hands grab hold of her ass, grinding my cock to her seam. I don't know how long I've got her plastered to me when the bell dings, but I can't contain the hunger much longer. I pull my mouth away from hers and carry her out of the elevator.

Hunting for the room number, she shouts, "This one right here."

Thank you, Hunter. It's the first door to the left of the elevators. I unlock the suite with the key card and slip right in, letting the door swing closed behind us without letting her go. The room is large, but I can't tell a damn thing about it because all my attention is on her. I need to get Maria naked and her thighs parted to take every inch of me until I release all my damn cum into her depths. There are no words to describe how painful it is to stare and not touch, not invade, not demand that every inch of her be mine.

"Take off your clothes, or I'll tear them off," I grunt out as I set her on her feet.

"You wouldn't," she says, shaking her head, challenging me.

"The hell I wouldn't." I reach toward her and grab her shirt and rip it off, buttons flying everywhere. She gasps, and I quickly remove her gun belt, setting it on the floor before pushing her onto the bed with her legs trapped between mine. Leaning over her, I whisper, "Care to challenge me on anything else?"

"You won't eat my pussy." My dick jerks, attempting to shred my jeans. She has no idea that there isn't anything I wouldn't do for her pleasure.

I laugh and shuck her pants off as inhumanly possible without hurting her. Her pink striped panties are soaked to the core with lust, and I rub my fingers along her slit with the fabric to add friction. Maria rolls her hips up, reaching for more as I breath in her scent, loving her arousal.

Nothing I've ever smelled could compare to the scent of my mate. I drag my mouth down her body, but she tenses. "You dared me." I adjust our bodies, tearing off the wet material, and then bump her legs open with my shoulders. "This is my pussy. You never keep it from me. Your scent is my addiction. You don't have to dare me to eat your pussy. I crave it more than anything." I press my face into her core, sliding my tongue along her lips. A low growl comes from deep inside me as my wolf takes insane pleasure in devouring my mate in the most hedonistic ways. I pump my tongue through her gooey sweetness, lapping up every single drop while driving her body to give me more. My queen lay there, thrashing her legs, unable to explain the pure lust consuming her as the first of many orgasms washes over her. I press my hand to her belly, holding her down as I go in for another orgasm. This time, I slip one finger into her tight sheath. There is nothing but us as I test her pussy, knowing that it's going to hurt her as I claim my mate. Teasing her, stretching her to another orgasm, I can no longer stave off my own need as I stalk up her body, staring at her as the tip of my cock brushes her folds. "Are you ready to be mine?"

"I've always been yours." It's all I need to hear as I slam my hips forward, plundering her warmth, marking her with my first load. My orgasm is quick and to the point, but I am nowhere near done with being sated. I have to have more of her. I pump in and out, steady strokes as I stare into her chocolate eyes. They glisten with unshed tears, but she's no longer in pain. She's greedily seeking another release from me, and I will gladly give them to her for the rest of our days. I pick up the pace, taking her mouth in a violent kiss, nipping at her bottom lip as we both go over the edge, coming again, and I fill her up with every drop of my seed. Tilting her head to the side, I bite down on her shoulder, marking, mating her. She cries out and so do I as the power of our union explodes around us, making us whole. Her womb hugs my cock, draining me again, and then I seal her mark with my tongue.

"Mine," I whisper.

She opens her eyes and smiles. "Yours."

We share another deep kiss before I pull away, holding my weight with my arms so it doesn't bear down on her, but she wraps herself around me, bringing me down. "It feels so good to have your weight on me."

"Baby, I'm a little too big to stay like this." We kiss gently before I pull out and fall to the side, dragging her with me. I close my eyes and fall fast asleep with her head on my chest.

4

Maria

I STARE DOWN at my mate. It's so weird to say, but I don't stop myself from thinking of him that way. I suppose my supernatural assumption was accurate and not me losing my mind. He's real, and he's here. I press my head into the crook of his shoulder and chest, feeling a profound sense of being home. *Was I ever this at peace?*

"I'm so glad you're at peace." *God, she's beautiful.*

"She who?" I hiss, sitting up in the bed.

"What?" He pushes himself up, leaning against the headboard.

"You said she's beautiful."

Can you hear me, Maria? I stare in amazement as his mouth doesn't move.

"Oh my goodness. I can hear you!"

"This is nuts. I need to talk to Hunter," he growls.

"Can you call him? I'm not ready for our time to end." *This has been magical.*

"It certainly has. Maria, it will never end. I'll want you all day. Although, I must say it's probably best that we return to White Wolf Ridge soon."

"I have a job here," I say, which is obvious because I was in full uniform when we met. I'm sure that it's in tatters somewhere around here.

"Yeah. I saw. You're a police officer. I can't say that I like that idea at all."

"Why?"

"The obvious reason, of course. It's fucking dangerous, and you're my mate."

"It isn't that dangerous."

"No? What happened to the sheriff a few years ago?"

"Well, that was a personal issue and like you said, a few years ago."

"I don't care. You're my mate. If you die, I will follow you."

"What?"

"Yes. We can't live without our other halves, and once they're gone, it doesn't take long for us to join them. I need to go back home. I'm sorry, but you have to come with me."

"I know. I'm not upset."

"You're lying to me. Look, I get it. It's not like I can be the one to uproot my life, but I'll promise to be the best mate, lover, husband, and friend you'll ever have."

"You're going to be busy, and I'm going to be alone." He cradles my face, stares into my eyes, and I feel his love flow through me.

"I'll always be there for you. You're my priority, Maria. Always."

"Anytime I need you?"

"Anytime you need me. I do have to tell you that we have a large ski resort with over four hundred rooms and twenty-five cabins that are my responsibility. I have a staff of two hundred different employees, and I'd love for you to take any part you want. If you really want to be a police officer, I'll replace the chief of police with you."

"What? You can do that?"

He gives me that killer smile that sets my body ablaze with lust. "As it happens, I can. My father's the mayor. Besides, the chief of police is a piece of shit."

"What has he done?" I question. I hate people who abuse their position.

"Nothing I care to talk about right now while I have you naked and in my arms," he whispers, and desire floods me, but then I think I probably smell. He has me pinned to the bed, grinding his cock along my seam.

"I need a shower," I plead, feeling filthy after our intense encounter.

"Then let's shower together," he growls, and I can get on board with that. I lift myself up and then he pulls me back down, covering my face in kisses. "I'm obsessed."

"So am I," I answer, rolling my hips upward to feel his length hit my pussy. He arches his brow and then takes me in one smooth pump, filling me deeply. We continue to rock back and forth until I cry out, my walls squeezing in waves of pleasure as his seed coats me and his roar resounds around the room.

I close my eyes and attempt to catch my breath while Turner lies on his back. "Maybe you should take a shower on your own or I'll end up getting inside your pussy again, and I'm sure it needs some rest."

"Okay," I sigh, panting still. This man makes me forget everything.

"Will it always be this way?"

"I sure the fuck hope so. Even after a half-dozen kids, I'll still chase you around the house."

"Six kids?"

"Well, it's not likely, but I hope to have a few."

"I'm just wondering what I'm in for."

"Whatever you want. You can take birth control, or we can avoid your ovulation cycle." He says as if it's no big deal, but it's too much for me at the moment.

"This is all too complicated. I'm going to wash up, and then I need some serious food."

The hotel room phone rings right on cue, and Turner answers it. "Hello. Yes. That would be great. Tomorrow would be good. Is there a way to get some food up here? Okay." He hangs up the phone and turns his head back to me. "That was Hunter. He offered to talk when we had time tomorrow. Also, he will send up a variety of foods."

"Then I better hurry and get...oh my. I don't have any clothes."

I'll text Mark and have him ask Hunter's mate or the other mate to pick up some clothes for you."

"Thank you."

"Anything for my queen." He winks, and I hurry into the shower. It's about ten minutes later when I wrap a fluffy white robe around my body. I step out into the room, and the food is there along with a shopping bag from the store downstairs.

"Cat sent that up for you. She said she figured you'd need a change of clothes." He hands me the note with his cheeks slightly pinkened. **If he's an animal, which we know he is, you'll need these. —Cat**

"That woman is a lifesaver."

"Eat first, and then you can get dressed." He takes a seat on the sofa with just his boxer briefs on, looking masculine and sexy.

"Sounds like a plan to me." I pick up a tray of fruit, and Turner pulls me onto his lap. I let out a gasping giggle and some of the berries land on me and all around us. "Bad boy."

"Give me a bite."

"I don't know if I feel like sharing," I tease. He snarls and snatches the plate from me. "Beast. Give me my berries."

"Only if you promise to share, my beauty."

"Okay. I promise." I pout, and he presses his lips to mine before giving me the plate back. I take a strawberry and put it to his lips and he quickly snaps his teeth, tearing the sweet red berry from my fingers. I watch his sexy lips as he chews, and then his thick column of a neck as he swallows. Damn, he's gorgeous. I lean in and steal a kiss from him, which is a huge mistake because I find myself pinned against the sofa with his mouth pushing my robe open and sucking on my nipples.

"So sexy, but I need to feed you." He sits up and helps me. "How about some eggs?"

"I could go for some." I stand, not caring that my robe is open as I grab a plate and then open the serving dish.

"Would you like some?" I ask when he comes to stand next to me.

"Thank you, but I can serve myself. You don't have to do that for me." He winks and grabs his own plate, scooping up his eggs. We make our plates and then take a seat at the dining table. This is one hell of a cool suite.

"Do you need anything, love?"

"No. This breakfast is so good." I eat like I've never eaten before. I suppose I've never been this hungry, and I know it's from all the exercise he's putting me through.

"I've had something that tastes so much better," he growls, leaning to kiss my cheek.

"Yes, but we both can't survive on sex." Just as I say that, his stomach rumbles.

"You got me there." With one more laugh, we eat in companionable silence. I steal glances at my mate, wondering how I've let myself fall so easily.

Because we are meant to be, my mate.

Then maybe we should get to know each other better.

We have a lifetime for that.

"Stop staring at my tits," I say out loud, giving him a pout to emphasize my point.

"It's nearly impossible when I can see your nipples." I look down, and my breasts are practically out of the robe. I grab my edges and adjust.

"Now, finish your food," I huff and then quickly take a bite of sausage to do my best not to laugh when a puppy-dog look spreads across his face. "Seriously."

He stops and takes my hands in his. "Am I pushing you too far, Maria? I've never felt like this before."

Seeing his pain isn't something I care for even just a

bit. Pulling my hands away from his only causes him to frown even more. I shake my head and then cup his face with both of my hands. "No. I think you're adorable."

"Adorable? I've never been called that before."

"Well, you are. Now eat, because I have a feeling that you don't eat like a bird and you have more rolls in the hay planned for the day."

"Yes, I just checked my schedule, and that seems to be all I have on the agenda. Sunup to sundown, it's all hay day." I shake my head and watch him eat again. Damn, my pussy's feeling all tingly, so I slam my legs closed.

"You know, you're no help. Do I have to eat in the other room, woman?"

"Um...might be a better idea." He shakes his head and turns around so I can't stare. He eats quickly as I finish my last few bites. I didn't put as much on my plate, so I finished first. After washing my hands, I dig into the bag Cat had brought up for me. I pull out two pairs of pants and underwear and bras with some cute boots and cozy socks.

"Ooh. These are so pretty and just my size." I know Cat and I are roughly the same build, although I'm a tad bit shorter.

"I'm glad it was Cat who picked them out, or I'd be really fucking angry," he growls, coming to see the red panties and matching bra.

"Grr. You're so sexy when you get territorial, as if someone else could possibly steal me away."

"They can try," he says just barely above a whisper. I grab his arm and turn him, although it's with his own power that he spins on his heel.

I look into his stunning eyes and say, "I'm not going anywhere."

"Good, because I'd chase your ass and bring you back," he growls, cupping the back of my head and dragging my lips to his.

I pull away and then attempt to bolt, but his strong arms create a steel band around me, slamming his front to my back. "Not so fast," he whispers, sliding his hand down the front of my body, down to the top of my thigh while the other wraps around my throat. "I'd love to give a good chase, and when I catch you, I'll be working your pussy out, making you scream over and over again until you can't take it anymore and then I'll push you again."

"Maybe I should get dressed before it gets any later," I say while grinding my ass on his cock.

"Yes because I don't think your pussy can handle any more penetration." He kisses my cheek and then pulls back. "It's time for me to go wash my ass. Get dressed before I'm tempted to fucking devour you all over again."

"Fine. What about your clothes?"

"I asked them to get my bag out of the SUV. The valet is bringing it up." The knock at the door is on time. He walks to the door in his pants without a shirt and takes the bag from the valet.

"Okay. Talk about having clout."

"It's what I expect out of a well-run resort. Hunter's got his game running smoothly."

"I think so. I loved their spa. I had such a great massage the other day."

And there goes his grunt and growl. "A massage? A woman or man?"

I roll my eyes at him and walk over to the bathroom. "A woman, of course. Seriously, go shower now." I hold open the bathroom door and wave to him to get inside.

The second he's in the shower, my phone goes off. It's Jacob. "Hey where are you?"

"I'm home. Where are you?"

"I'm not home. I have some things going on, and well...I just can't talk about them at the moment."

"What's going on? You're not on duty, are you?"

"No. I'm not, but I'm out. Sorry, I have to go." I end the call, sitting on the bed, feeling unsure. I nearly said I found my mate. I almost let the truth slip out. I have to be more careful, but isn't Jacob a shifter as well?

I slip on the panties and the bra. I stand up and look in the large mirror on the dresser. The cup size is a little small, but the width is just fine. Although now it looks like I could pose for those provocative photoshoots. I stare at myself and smile. I look good. My hair's down, falling over my shoulders, framing my face perfectly.

I drop my head and pose. Then I decided to climb on the bed and kneel with my legs spread out, posing for the imaginary camera. A low rumble comes from the bathroom. *Can you see me?*

No, but I can feel your arousal. Interesting. The bathroom door opens and before I know it, Turner's on me, lifting me, crushing his mouth to mine and then tossing me onto the mattress.

He pulls back, resting on his calves as he drags my panties off. "Hey, don't ruin them."

"I'm not. They're sexy as fuck on you." I reach around and pop the clasp on the bra, pulling it off to watch his eyes darken. He bends down and sucks on my nipple, biting on it. I let out a moan so loud that I surprise myself.

"Wow, calm down, tiger."

"Tiger? I'm a wolf."

"Tiger, wolf—same difference," I scoff, knowing he's going to get aggressive. My body burns to feel that intensity on and in me.

"I'll show you a difference." He flips me onto all fours and then slides his cock deep inside me. I cry out from the fullness and then he pulls back, nearly completely out, but then slams back home.

"Fuck," I hiss, needing more. I need his touch and he gives it to me, sliding his hands up and down my back before moving them to my front and cupping my breasts and thrusting violently, the sound of our flesh slapping resounding through the room. It doesn't take long for our sweaty bodies to come. I shake as he wraps himself around me, his head to my neck as he pumps every last drop inside of me.

We stay on our knees for a minute longer and then he falls to the side, taking me with him as he spoons me. "Sleepy," I yawn.

"Rest, my queen."

5

Turner

WE'VE LAID down and made love more times than I can count in the past twenty-four hours, but I must get back to White Wolfe before the new season kicks off. I took a quick shower and now I'm dressed and ready to leave, but it's time to wake up my mate.

I call out to her because I know if I touch her, I'll lose control again. "Love, we're supposed to meet with Hunter and Cat downstairs in his office in about an hour."

"Okay," she says groggily, turning onto her side with her ass in my line of sight. Fuck, I need to keep my dick down for a bit or we'll be late to everything.

"Maria, come on. Get in the shower and get dressed." She never managed to put on more clothes, so she still has the ones Cat gave her.

"Fine." She slides off the bed, completely naked with tiny marks from my hands and mouth. She pads off like a grumpy little thing, which makes me smile. We need to get home, and then she can sleep all she wants.

I have a hundred messages. Mostly a bunch of congratulations. I have to call my father, who wants to hear from me.

I call him first to see what he has to say. Since I didn't personally inform anyone but my brother, I'm sure he's probably not too pleased with me. "Hey there, son. I wondered when I'd hear from you. How is everything with your mate?"

"It's great. We're getting everything prepared to come home tomorrow."

"That's good news. I can't wait to meet her. What can you tell us? Your mother has been waiting to hear news, and so has the rest of the pack. Everywhere I go, I get asked about the new Alpha female."

"There's a lot I'm still working out. I have no idea where Mark is at the moment. I should check with him since he sent me a text as well. I kind of ditched him with the Alpha here when I found my mate."

"I have heard from him. He's having a good time hanging out, but he's waiting on your call. I know you're busy, but let me know if you need any help."

"Thanks, Dad. Maria and I are going down to meet with the Alpha, Hunter, and his mate today before we plan our next steps."

"So Maria's her name? You haven't mentioned anything about your mate."

"That's because, well, it seems my mate is human."

"Human? Really?"

"Yes."

"Well, that's interesting. I hadn't expected that."

"Me either. That's why we're going to talk to Hunter and his mate, who is also a human."

"Well, then, it seems that it is not as uncommon as I believed."

"Are you upset, Dad?"

"Why would I be? As long as she's your mate, nothing else matters. I am certain that she is perfect for you."

"Thank you, Dad. I've got to go, but I'll talk to you later." I end the call and stare at my mate with just a towel wrapped around her body. "Beautiful."

"Don't even think of it, mister. We have to get ready for our meeting, and there's still a thousand things to do before we leave Wolfe Creek."

"Are you okay with leaving here?"

"It's going to be a little sad, but it's not like we're far away. Besides, my roots aren't here. I go where you go, and that's White Wolf."

"Get dressed before I take your sweet ass again."

"I don't think I've ever been called sweet before."

"Well, you are." I stand up and adjust my erection so I can actually take a step. This is such a new and weird experience for me. I hadn't thought of this issue before, but I suppose I should get used to it.

She takes her clothes and walks back into the bathroom, which I think is a great idea so this fucker can go down before we go downstairs.

Five minutes later, I've calmed and my erection has settled to half-mast, which is the best I can hope for. She comes out, looking elegant in a pair of jeans and a pretty button-down top. It's light blue and hugs her large breasts. I do my best to get my jealousy under control. It's just a blouse, for heaven's sake.

"Are you ready?"

"Yes. Everything feels nice. I have to ask her where she gets her clothes."

"Well, you look perfect. Let's go." I take her hand and lead her out of our room and wait for the elevators. There's another couple there and the woman eyes my mate with a critical eye, and I want to beat her man's ass because I won't touch a woman.

"Excuse me? Is there something wrong with my outfit? You're staring with disgust."

"No. I wasn't looking at you like that."

"I can see your reflection. Either way, we'll be taking this elevator down alone."

I lose it when I realize why the woman's upset with Maria. It's because her bastard man is staring at Maria's breasts. I'm on him in a second, ready to rip his fucking head off. I slam him against the wall, pinning him there while I snarl and my wolf demands to be let out. "Turner? Calm down."

"No. There's a reason his wife is jealous of you. He was just checking you out."

"He's not worth it. Come, love. It's a pity that not all men are like you." I let him go because my queen wants me to, but I give him a warning look. I could kill him with my bare hands, and he has no fucking idea. I take a deep breath, and the elevator doors finally open. We get inside while he shoves off his wife's hands as she tries to care for him. I'll be having a talk with Hunter about that. I sense a domestic fight about to happen.

"You are so sexy when you're territorial like that. I was almost tempted to let you pummel him, but I was afraid your wolf would have come out."

"It's a close one. I'm glad I have you to calm me down. Although, I don't ever remember being that murderous. Even as teen, I never had the urge to kill someone."

"Well, let's try to keep that to a minimum. Okay?"

"I'll do my best. You're my mate and therefore an extension of me. Disrespect to you is a direct disrespect to me."

"Understood. Now, let's just talk to our hosts so we can go back and you can fuck that anger out," she purrs against my ear before kissing my cheek.

I let out a growl. "Damn, baby. You're killing me. I still haven't gotten this fucker under control."

"Sorry." She giggles as the elevator doors open up, but there's a small group of people waiting to get on and I don't miss the way several women stare at my privates.

"He's mine, ladies," Maria hisses with a flick of her hair. I lead her to the front desk.

"Hello, miss. We're looking for Mr. Wolfe's office."

"Mr. and Mrs. Turner, please go through that hallway and to your right. He's expecting you."

"Thank you." I nod and take Maria's hand as we walk across the library. My ears are pricked, and I know that we need to give them a minute. "Apparently they've lost track of time." We both laugh and then hear the sound of clothes rustling.

"Maria." I turn around to hear the man who called my woman. It's Sheriff Erik, coming toward us in his full uniform. "Turner," he adds. "I'm surprised you managed to find time to talk to Hunter. I had to make him drag me out of bed almost quite literally."

"Well, thank goodness he didn't try because I'd have to kill him."

"Yeah, well, luckily, I'm married to his sister."

"Very true."

"I just wanted to say congratulations, and I haven't told the station yet, but I'm assuming that you're leaving with him to White Wolf Ridge, correct?"

"Yes. I'm sorry."

"No. Don't be sorry. I understand more than just about anyone. I'm happy that everything worked out." He smiles and extends his hand to me. "I'm sure I don't have to tell you to be good to her, but don't fuck up." He winks and gives her a handshake before turning on his heel. I like the man, although it helps that he's a shifter and already mated.

The office door opens, and Hunter greets us. "It's good see you down here, Turner, Maria. Please come in."

"Thank you." It's clear that they just fucked like rabbits, but I'm not going to address it. It's pointless to bother, making them uncomfortable.

"Thank you for coming. I'm so happy for you. Hunter and I wanted to give you guys kind of the rundown of how this whole Alpha-human thing works. We've been kind of learning as we go along and making notes because we know that we're not the only ones and there's a possibility for more to come in the future."

"Please, take a seat." When we do, Hunter pulls Cat onto his lap and she starts talking. "Now, the reason your wolf picked a human is simply because you're the strongest of your pack and thus can handle being mated to a human, but I think you should ask any questions you have. Do you have any questions for us?"

"A huge one, actually. Will she become a shifter as well?"

"Yes, but it doesn't always happen right away. One of the biggest things that causes a human to change is something happening to your mate. From the readings of our ancestors, it didn't happen until after she had their first child, but for us, it was when our former Beta attacked us," Hunter says with a snarling anger, reliving the memory.

"And it's strange, but I can hear her thoughts as clear as day."

"And vice versa," Maria adds.

"Another benefit of the Alpha-human connection. It helps in times of danger and strengthens the bond."

"The pups?"

"Our babies will be just like any other shifter pup." *I'll explain any questions you have about our pups later.*

"Wow. Okay, so it's pretty much the same except the whole hearing thoughts kind of thing," I say, attempting to be under control, but I'm still riled up and hearing pups makes me harder than fuck.

"That's very good to know," Maria says.

"And before we leave, I have to say I had a little argument with one of your guests."

"A little argument? Like slamming up against the wall?" he questions with a smirk. How was he aware of that so fast? "I have cameras and saw the entire incident. I'll keep an eye on them. I'm surprised you were able to back away. After watching the surveillance video, you were right to beat him if you wanted. He noticed her yesterday and said he wanted his wife to have an ass like that."

"What?"

"Well, I've already had my security escort them out of the hotel. Trust me, I understand more than anyone what mating does to us, but they're regular humans and they don't live by our moral standards."

"I'm only letting it go because I'd rather be home with my mate then finding ways to shred the fucker apart."

"Good. So, if you have any questions, feel free to give us a call. Here are our private cells." He hands me the card. "We'll let you get back to doing what you need."

"I need to get her back home. Thank you for the stay." We shake hands, and the girls hug each other.

We go upstairs, and as soon as that door closes I have her pinned to it, pants down and panties pushed to the side before slamming into her. "You look sexy as fuck like this, mate. Your pussy was throbbing in the room. Did it make you horny to think of having my babies?"

"Yes," she moans, resting her head back on my shoulder.

"I could feel it. I'm just making sure I got the job done. I can't wait to see you round, belly swollen, breasts full, letting everyone know that you belong to me. Understand, Maria? You belong to me."

"Yes, Alpha."

I do my best to maintain control. The word from her lips goes straight to my wolf. He wants her submission, and she's given it. "Good, remember that. Remember that when your pussy needs me, demand satisfaction."

"Fuck, ah," she cries, her warmth holding my cock in a death grip.

"That's right. Come on my cock while I breed you," I growl, biting her bared neck. Her walls convulse, orgasming as I roar out my seed deep into her, marking her again.

"I love when you bite me."

"I love having my mark all over you." I pull out of her and let her feet hit the floor. The door vibrates as we take our weight off it. I'm sure the fucker shook as I possessed my mate, but I heard nothing but her pleasure and mine.

I reach over and adjust her panties, fitting them into place, feeling our sticky release on my fingers. She turns and quickly sucks my fingers into her mouth. I growl and push her down to her knees. "Since you like to clean me off, mate, your Alpha needs you to clean off my cock."

"Your mate wants to lick you clean," she says, her eyes brightened, heated as she wraps her hand around my length. Her lips part as she takes the tip and slides it between them until it's disappeared into her mouth. Unable to control the pleasure, I cup her head and start letting go, fucking her like the beast I am. I let off and pull out, feeling like I'm a bit too rough with my queen, but she grabs hold. "I'm not done. I need you, my Alpha."

"Fuck. You asked for it, my queen." I lock my fist around her hair and tilt her head up as I push my cock deep into her mouth. "It's yours, baby. Take it."

"I'm going to come," she cries out, but I need to feel it, so I pop out of her mouth and scoop her up and toss her on the bed. Pouncing on top of her with a hurried need, my tip nudges her entrance as I push her legs open wide. I grab hold of that waste of material and shred it.

"I'll buy you hundreds more for me to shred," I promise before plundering her womb in and out, hooking the backs of her knees over my arms as I kneel and punish her pussy. "I'll never get enough," I grunt, causing her to splinter and come hard, shaking wildly as I fill her up again with every fucking drop.

It takes another hour to get ourselves under control enough to leave the hotel. We grab our things from the room because we don't plan to return. Soon, I'll have her in our home, filling her womb in every damn room in the house until neither of us can walk. Fuck, I can barely manage it now. Maybe she's right; I should have eaten more than a meager meal and her pussy. We step out of the room and make it down to the valet to get my truck without me pulling her back inside. Waiting outside with my queen's hand in mine, I breathe in the chilly air and smile. I'm a happy son of a bitch.

My SUV pulls up and the guy steps out, nodding to me before nodding respectfully to my mate. I hand him a tip. I can tell he's a shifter too, and young. "Come on. We have to go to your apartment and at the very least pack your clothes, mate." I kiss her cheek and then open the passenger door when I really want to slam her against the SUV and bang her fucking brains out again. This lust has me in a haze.

"I'll drive," she says, walking away from the open door. "You don't know where I live. So please don't argue. Also, we need to find your Beta."

"Shit. That's the second time I forgot to contact him." Taking her sunglasses from the bag Cat gave her, Maria slips them over her gorgeous eyes. She switches gears and pulls out like a professional driver. Fuck, she looks hot with all that confidence that pours from her. Shaking my head, I finally remember what I need to do, and I say, "Call Mark."

"Calling Mark," the car says back.

"Oh my goodness. I forgot about my brand-new, many-monthly-payments-to-go Chevy Silverado."

"We can have him bring it back, and I'll have it paid off by the end of the week. Just make sure to remind me."

It rings twice, and he answers. "Hey, you remembered about me!"

"Yeah, well, when you find your mate, you can take a day or two off. Where are you?"

"At your mate's apartment, hanging out with her roommate. He seems like a cool guy." Mark's a much calmer being than me, which makes him a great Beta. He's tough when he needs to be but usually has a calm, cool demeanor and gets along with everyone.

"We're almost there," I snarl, hating that he's fraternizing with the man who lives with my mate. It's stupid, but I feel the beast in me tense up.

"Ugh. This man. Anyway. We'll be there in five minutes. Bye," Maria says before ending the call on me. She turns her eyes on me for a moment and says, "Hey, I'm going to tell you now. Be nice to Jacob. He has never looked at me in any way but a roommate."

"I know he isn't interested. After all, he's a shifter just like me. I shouldn't be jealous, but I am."

"Isn't he the reason you're down here in the first place?"

"Yes."

"So we wouldn't have met..." I know what she's getting at, but my wolf doesn't like that one bit and the man in me feels a straining pain in my chest at that idea.

"That's not acceptable. Don't even think it."

"I'm just saying. You owe him."

"He and I are even," I state, willing to give only that.

"So no fighting."

"Fine, but keep the hugs to a minimum. And when I say minimum, I mean none."

"Okay, crazy. He and I have never hugged." She pulls into the apartment parking lot and then turns off the engine, rolling her eyes in the process. *I'm possessive. I can't and won't deny it—ever.*

It's hot, except when it's against someone I think well of.

"Good to know." I step out and walk around, looking for any trouble. I don't see or sense any, but I crowd my mate anyway. There's no way in hell I'll let anyone harm a hair on her pretty head.

"Here are your keys," she says, dumping them in my hand.

We go into the apartment building and up to the second floor. Mark opens the door for us. "Why, hello, Alpha."

"Thank you for so kindly inviting me into my own home," Maria states.

"Sorry."

"I'm teasing." She smiles at Mark. "I'm sorry we

weren't properly introduced." She steals a glance at me, waiting for me to do it.

"Mate, this is my Beta, Mark Keats," I say. "Mark, this is your Alpha female, Maria."

"It's a pleasure to meet his second in command."

"You are now my second," I tell her. She holds more power than she knows or maybe even understands, but she will one day.

"He's right. I'm now third. The third wheel." He winks, and then we hear noise in the kitchen.

"Jacob," I call out, causing Mark to step to the side. "How are you?" I look, and you can't tell he has any markings on him.

"Wow." *He doesn't look like he got into a fight.*

"We heal a lot faster," I tell her.

"Oh." *I need to take notes.*

"I can't believe you've mated with him," he huffs with a tone that makes me want to rip his throat out.

"Him?" I snarl. "If I were you, I'd watch your tone. If my sister is your mate, I'll make your life a living hell." I'm nearly in his face, and he takes a step back. The soft feel of Maria's hand on my forearm is the only reason I don't lunge at him to teach him some manners.

"He's got a point."

"Sister? What do you mean?" It takes her a minute. I never gave her details about the incident.

"That's why I came here. He kissed my sister. As the Alpha, I can't just let things go without looking weak," I inform her.

"It was just a kiss on the cheek to keep that scummy fucking human away from her," Jacob spits out in disgust, as if the image is planted in his brain. Having my mate by my side, I understand that the thought of another close to her would send me into a rage.

"I get it, but I have to do my job as the Alpha."

"Well, I've got a year, and then I'll be back in White Wolfe. She's my mate, and I know it."

"What makes you so sure?"

"I feel it in my soul. I felt her before I saw her."

"They said you might, but you need to stay away from her until the time's right. I don't think you can control yourself."

"What difference does it make? It's not like I can make her mine until then," he hisses out, popping a seat on the sofa.

"Because you'll be challenging everyone who breathes near her, and that's a risk I'm not willing to allow. I'm betting that if you had your way, the little fuck flirting with her would disappear permanently."

"You guessed right."

"Only if you promise to protect her. I refuse to be afraid that something's going to happen to her." I sense the tension in him.

"Why don't you come back and work with us?" I look at Mark like he's nuts, but he just continues. "That way you can keep an eye on Aria while still keeping your distance and getting to know her."

"What happens if they aren't mates then?" I remind my Beta, who's offering up a future in our town.

"Then I'll leave," Jacob sighs. There's resignation in his tone, reassuring me, but I still have to get clarification so there's no misunderstanding.

"You promise?"

"On my life."

"It will be."

"Fine. Just remember—you don't touch her again until that mating kicks in. You better hope she's your mate."

"Turner," Maria warns me. I grab her and plant my mouth on her lips.

"Yes, my sweet?"

"Relax. I'm going to go pack."

"I'm coming with you."

"How about you sit down? Organize who is going to take my truck to White Wolf. I'll go and deal with getting my things organized. I'll do my best to hurry." She kisses my cheek and leaves us guys to talk. I miss her already, but she's got to get shit together. I'll only come if she needs me or takes too long for my liking.

"So you can take Maria's vehicle back home."

"It's still at the police station. We can go pick it up and grab her things from her locker there—that way it's all squared away. I'm not on duty until tonight, so I can drop you off right before I start my shift," Jacob offers.

"That sounds good."

"You want a beer?" Mark asks.

"No, thanks. I need a sober head. This mating thing has got me fucked up. I nearly fucked up some human at the resort. The motherfucker was staring at Maria's ass."

"Humans," they say simultaneously.

I hear a sigh come from the bedroom, and I'm already three steps toward the door. "I need boxes."

"I have them in the other room. I'll set them by the door," Mark says.

"Good."

I'm coming, baby.

You don't have to.

You're my queen. I am your servant.

I walk in, and she looks tired. Two suitcases are zipped up and I grab them, testing the weight. No wonder she's exhausted. They're stuffed. "How much more do you want to take?"

I look around the room and see a bunch of photos and personal items. "I'm assuming I don't need to bring any of the furniture, right?"

"Yes."

"Then I'll need a few more boxes, and I'll have all my things." I pull her into my arms, rubbing her back as she rests her head on my chest.

"Okay." There's a knock at the door, causing her to pull back slightly.

"Alpha, we'll leave the boxes by the door."

"What?"

"Mark knew you'd need to pack up and had boxes brought here for you."

"Smart man." I let out a low growl. My mating heat hasn't worn off, and even complimenting another man sends me into a possessive mood.

"Josiah," she says.

"Leave us," I snarl. We hear footsteps and then the front door opens and closes.

"I need you now." I pin her to the bed and forget everything else for the next half hour.

6

Turner

We finally get on the road to White Wolf Ridge around six at night. The sun's down, but with my keen eyesight, I don't have to worry about the darkness. Once we reach the outskirts of Wolfe Creek, the light fades and the only things to light the way are the moon and our headlights. Maria's calm by my side, but I sense her fatigue kicking in. I know that our loving will have to wait until she rests.

We arrive at our home, and I see the sign up on the porch. A large banner reads *Congratulations Josiah and Maria.* Then, I spot my father, mother, and siblings. Shaking my head, I silently apologize to Maria as she frowns.

Oh shit. What if they don't like me?

They will love you. I promise. If they don't, I'll send them out of my pack.

She gasps, and I laugh.

"Jerk."

"I'm your jerk." I lean over and kiss her cheek.

I step out of the SUV and so does Maria, so I quickly move to her side and lead her toward my family and our home.

"Oh my goodness, she's a doll," my mother, Adaline, blurts out, coming forward to hug Maria. She's startled at first, but then relaxes. *I told you so.*

"Enough, woman. Let the poor little thing go." My mother reluctantly releases my mate. I pull Maria toward me and give the slightest growl so that the men keep their distance. My mother's one thing. The rest can get lost.

"Good boy. It's a pleasure to meet you. We just couldn't help ourselves. Turner's been waiting for you to come into his life."

"Well done, brother," Max says, clapping my back while smiling at my mate. I want to snarl and tell him to back off, but he isn't doing anything wrong and is the least harmless person to my mate except for myself.

"Thank you, although I can't take credit for fate stepping in to find my love. Mother, Father, Max, Aria, this beautiful creature is my mate, Maria. Now, if you all will excuse us, we need to go inside and get settled. You're welcome to stay, but Max, I could use some help bringing her things inside."

"Okay." We walk inside and there are balloons everywhere, and I smell food in the oven.

"Thank you, Mother and Aria." I tilt my head toward them.

"You're welcome. The men will go and get Maria's things. Shoo. Us girls need to chat."

Are you okay with that?

Yes.

I nod and walk back outside. "Where's Mark?"

"He's bringing Maria's vehicle back from Wolfe Creek. He should be getting home in a few hours."

"So tell us. How does it feel to be mated to a human?" Max says. There's something in his tone that's hard to figure out. Is there longing?

"I suppose the same as being mated to a shifter. Although I wouldn't know."

"You talked to the Alpha in Wolfe Creek?"

"Yes, Hunter Wolfe. He and his wife are extremely happy and still going at it daily over the past few years."

"That bodes well. Normally the mating slows down and the need lightens," my father says.

"Yes, well, not for them, and I sure as fuck hope not for us. Take this, and I'll take these," I tell my brother. My father grabs the last box and says, "Are these all of her belongings?"

"Yes. She doesn't need the rest of the stuff, so her roommate can keep it. Fucking hell, the roommate." I shake my head, chuckling to myself.

"What about the roommate?" Max asks.

"You won't believe who he is."

"Who?"

"The guy you roughed up for kissing Aria."

"And you didn't rip his head off?" He looks pissed.

"What for? He was no threat to Maria."

"Still."

"No. Still. Do we have to go over this again? I'm not interested in a war with people over something so damn inconsequential. Add on to the fact that he was attempting to protect Aria from some stupid human. We might not like that she's almost of mating age and so is that young man, but it's the way of things. If they're mated, then so be it. He'll be family, so you need to get over it."

"Fine."

"What's wrong with you?"

"I hate this whole thing about mates and forever with just one person. I can't even choose the person. Life does it for me."

"Who is she?" My father beats me to the question.

"Who is what?" Max looks offended, tension flooding his body. I don't like it, but I remain his brother and not the Alpha. He doesn't need that right now.

"Who is the lady that you're interested in that clearly isn't for you?" I ask.

"There's no lady or anything. I just hate the idea of not choosing."

"I'm sorry you feel that way, but you need to remember some people search their entire lives to find someone who may love them enough. We're fortunate to have someone that brings us pure desire, need, love," my father adds before heading into the house.

I stay back and watch my brother shake his head.

"I can't see it that way. I hate to do this, but I'm leaving town. I'm going to college out of state and far away from here, so I don't have to deal with this bullshit."

"That's fine, Max. Does Dad know of your wishes?"

"He does. We talked about it. Are you sure you're okay with it? You're the Alpha, after all? You can't have us defecting."

"I love you, Max, which means I want your happiness. If that means moving away and going to school somewhere where you can be your own man, that's fine. I'll make sure you have what you need, but I'll only be a call away."

"Thank you, bro." We head into the house and set the boxes upstairs in our bedroom. Once we come downstairs, the women are giggling in the kitchen.

"You all better not be laughing about me," I grumble, sliding my hands over Maria's hips.

"Nope," Aria says quickly, shoving a grape in her mouth to avoid saying anything, but she can hardly hide the smile on her face.

I toss my head back and groan. Being the Alpha means nothing to my family. "Let me guess. The time I first shifted?"

"You were adorable. I told you," Maria whispers.

"Dinner's almost done. Why don't you set the plates... all of you men?"

"Come on. We're getting the boot again."

"It's cool, because after dinner I'm kicking you all out."

"We get it. You want to get your mate alone," Aria says, rolling her eyes. I take a stack of plates, and my dad grabs the silverware. We start setting it up in the dining room when my phone rings.

"Hey, Hunter. What's up?"

"That fuckhead wants to sue you and me. I'm just giving you a heads up. I've already scratched the tape and since no one called the Sheriff's office to call in a disturbance, they've got nothing."

"I should have killed the prick."

"Nah—then you'd have to take time away from your mate. Have fun. I squashed it, and they've left my hotel for good."

"Thanks. Take care."

"You, too."

"What the hell was that about?"

"Some human had the nerve to ogle my mate and then roughed around his woman, so I threatened him."

"You attacked someone over your mate? See, mating made you fucking stupid and careless. I can't deal with this shit. You acted petty, just like the humans. I'm out."

"Max," I call out, but he storms from the house.

"Let him go," my father says, gripping my shoulder hard, knowing that I'm tempted to run after him. I hear his vehicle speed out of my driveway way too damn fast.

"He's been a mess lately. Come on. Let's get some food in you and calm your woman and mine. I'm sure they're worried."

Are you okay?

I'm fine.

Liar.

I drop my head and hold on to the back of the dining room chair. I feel her hands slide around my waist. "I'm sorry," she says against my spine.

"You heard?" I whisper.

"I don't think there's anyone that didn't hear. It's not your fault. He needs time to figure out what he wants in life, even if it's hard to see him leave."

"Thank you, my love." I take her hand and bring it to my lips for a kiss.

"Let's go back to getting dinner ready. Your parents are worried, and your sister's upset."

"Of course." I spin around and pull her in for a kiss. "Thank you, my love."

"I'm so glad you don't feel that way about me."

"I was hoping to find my mate. Max is young. He wants a different life. That might still mean he can live in a major city and have a mate. I don't know how he'll be able to run wild in the city, but if that's what he wants, I have no problem."

We head into the kitchen, and my sister's crying.

"Why does he have to be so hotheaded?" she sobs.

"Calm yourself. He's going to college and he'll see that life isn't everything he thinks it is, and maybe he'll come back or maybe he finds his happiness out there." I lean in and pull my little sister into a hug.

"He's going to be okay. Do you know where he plans to go?" Maria asks.

"He wants to go to the University of Florida," my father answers, pulling the ribs out of the oven.

"Wow. He's doing his best to forget our way of life," I say, feeling like I'm failing as the Alpha. He didn't come to me to tell me his problems until he was ready to run.

"I did that when I was his age. I once lived in El Paso, Texas. I couldn't stand the heat, so I left as soon as I could. I visit my family on occasion, but I love it where I am now, and I wouldn't have met Turner if I didn't."

She's already acting like an Alpha female and trying to improve the spirits of her pack. "You have a good point. We just need to have faith. As the Alpha of the pack, I've given him my blessing to leave. As a father, you have as well."

"Yes, so we just need to support him," my father agrees.

"Now—enough of the misery. Let's eat. I'm starving," Aria says. She lets her wolf out a lot, running miles at a time every single morning before the sun is up. No one dares mess with her since she's the daughter of the former Alpha, but I know she needs to feel the breeze on her face and it's probably why she can out-eat everyone in this house. She burns so much energy that it makes me tired.

We gather everything needed and carry the trays and drinks to the dining room. I sit at the head of the table, and Maria's on my right so I can touch her whenever I need. Aria's on my left and my father is beside her, leaving my mother next to Maria.

"So, Maria, how many siblings do you have?" Aria asks as she takes half a slab of ribs and puts them on her plate. I take the tray from her and offer some to my mate, who takes only three small pieces. I grab a full slab for myself. I need as much food as I can before my father reaches out and grabs the tray to serve my mother. He loves to do such a small but loving gesture. She smiles up at him, grabbing her own half slab.

"I have two brothers who are married, and eight nieces and nephews."

"Really? That's crazy." I feel bad that I haven't even bothered to ask about her family.

It's okay. I wasn't interested in talking about my family. Only making a new one.

"Do you all get along?" my mother asks as she passes the potatoes.

Maria takes them and adds a large dollop to her plate before handing them to me. "Yes, but since I've moved away, I tend to talk to them less often."

"So you're like me. One girl, two brothers. I wonder if that's what you two will have."

"There's a possibility of that, but we have a long time before we need to worry about that."

"Not really, sweetheart. We have a shorter gestation period than normal humans," my mother adds in her expertise.

"Oh, goodness."

"Oh yes, I forgot to mention my mother's the local OBGYN for both humans and shifters."

"Although I do have to say I don't have experience with a human shifter baby."

"I'm going to have to call Cat Wolfe for that. They have several kids. Sorry—pups."

"No, that's fine, dear. Call them what you will. Most of the time we refer to them as children. With humans around, we must be careful," my mother says, reaching over and patting Maria's hand.

"There's so much to learn."

"It's okay. Take your time. Soon it'll come so naturally that you'll believe you were born a shifter."

"I do hope so."

"You will, or you wouldn't have made the perfect match for the Alpha." My sister makes a great point. Maria's the best woman to be mine for the rest of my days.

We eat dinner and talk about the basics. Aria's already planning a spa day with Maria, but I don't mind one bit. I want them to get along. I really want my brother to be here and be happy for me, but he needed to find his own path. My gut tells me he'll be back and that he just needs time. He wouldn't be the first to leave and go to college or live life before settling down in White Wolf.

It's nearly nine when we're done eating, and everyone takes the dishes and helps clean up. "We're going to leave you kids to have some time together. I know you still have to go back to work in the morning."

"Yes. I have to show Maria around and get the hang of everything before Daphne pops."

"So true." We exchange hugs, and they leave us to our own devices. I lock up the house and then turn to my queen.

"Mate. It's time for bed."

"Time for bed?" she raises her brow, attempting to toss the sexy look my way, but she can't hide the yawn that follows.

"Yes. To. Bed. You need sleep, my darling." I swiftly swing her into my arms and turn off the lights downstairs as I carry her to our bedroom. Everything can wait until tomorrow. My woman needs her rest. Stripping her down, I do my best to keep my arousal at bay and then slide one of my T-shirts over her body.

"I have a nightgown somewhere," she mutters.

"I know, but I like seeing you in my shirts." I lift her up, and she wraps her legs around me as we go into the bathroom and handle our nighttime routine. "Here you go." It's a pink toothbrush that matches mine. "I've been dreaming about you for six months, so I started grabbing random things that we'd both need when I went to the store."

"It's perfect. You're perfect and adorable." After we brush, I carry my sleepy woman to bed, tucking her in and then cradling her to my side. I've never felt so damn content, and sleep comes in a heartbeat.

7

Maria

WE WAKE UP SUPER EARLY, so early the sun isn't even out, and Turner's already on the phone with his mother. He's pacing back and forth as the tension rips through him. His assistant just went into labor, and there's still a few last-minute issues to be handled.

I stand in his path so he's forced to stop or collide with me. When he finally does pump the brakes, I offer my services. "I can help wherever you need. As of right now, I'm kind of unemployed."

He pulls me close and presses a kiss to the crown of my head and then tips my chin to look at him. "Thank you, but you're not unemployed. You own an entire ski resort. I can use your help, going over her notes and making sure the checklist she has is completed. Daphne's an extremely organized person, so it's all in one place, neatly updated every few hours."

"Okay. I'm sure I can manage just fine. Let's get ready

and to work before we get carried away with other things," I whisper, rubbing his growing erection. Hell, I'm not sure if he's ready to go all the time or not. I'm going to have to pay attention. Even that thought has me horny as hell again.

"I want to get carried away with you, Maria, but I do have to go to work and I could really use your help. I feel terrible putting this on you. You're supposed to be resting."

"I know we haven't been getting much sleep, but we will tonight." I climb out of bed and slip on my robe before going into the bathroom. I'm not trying to get him riled up. The second he sees too much skin, he's instantly aroused. I wash quickly, brushing my teeth and hair before he has a chance to run a hole in the floor with his pacing.

When I step out, he's in a nice suit that does dirty things to my girly parts and I do my best to control my inner thoughts, but I'm too late.

"After we get everything straightened out, I'm going to have you bent over my desk, filling you up with my suit still on."

"Okay. Well, until then, could you please make some coffee, and I'll get dressed."

"Sure thing, love." He winks and then leaves our room while I let out a long sigh. I wonder if I can block my thoughts from him.

Don't try it, woman.

It would help to curb our hunger at work.

True, but I always want to know what you're thinking.

I get ready and leave our bedroom without thinking

about anything but the process of getting dressed and a hot cup of coffee.

"Here's your cup. We have a few minutes to drink them, but I need to get an early start since Daphne's out."

"Understand. I'll follow your lead." He kisses my temple and then goes back to drinking his coffee.

His phone rings, and he grumbles before answering it. I know he'd rather spend time with me, so he's a bit grumpy. Finishing my coffee, I rinse out the cup and set it in the strainer, only to feel Turner's arms slide around me. "Are you ready, my love?"

"As I'll ever be." He takes my hand, and we put on our winter coats before heading out of the house. Strangely, I don't feel as cold as I should.

"I have a question."

"Shoot."

"I actually haven't seen your wolf. Are you like a type of arctic wolf?"

"I am definitely the type of wolf that can handle the cold. I love to run my paws into the cold snow. If you're not too tired tonight, I'll show you."

"Do you ski?" I ask, wanting to know more while avoiding the fact that he's so sexy. He holds up his hand and then closes the passenger door. I watch as he adjusts his cock through his slacks under his coat. I giggle to myself.

"Yes, and you?" he asks as he jumps in the driver's seat.

"I've never done it before."

"Maybe we'll get some time, and I can show you."

"That would be good," I choke out, immediately

feeling uncomfortable about the heights. I've never climbed the mountains in Wolfe Creek because I was scared.

"Are you afraid?"

"No... Maybe a little," I admit with pursed lips.

"Don't worry. I have great reflexes, and I won't let anything happen to you." He leans in and kisses my lips before turning on the SUV.

"Then I'm all yours."

"That you are." He pulls out of his driveway, and we're on our way to work. I'm super nervous, but I do my best to take it easy and think about how beautiful the snow looks against the lush greenery.

We drive through the mountain pass and arrive at a palatial-looking resort. Hunter's is nice, but this is much grander. Its entrance is like Wolfe's Den, but with a longer roundabout for the valet. He pulls into a spot where a few cars are actually parked, and it has his name on it. We exit and he takes my hand, leading me past all the curious eyes. He ignores everyone unless they greet us with a good morning. Then we walk down the hall and to the elevators. Off to the side is one that says Conference level. He presses the button for that elevator and the doors open immediately. "My office is on the top floor. It's where we have conference rooms for our guests," he answers my unspoken question.

"So that's the opposite of Wolfe's Den, then."

"Is that a bad thing?"

"Not at all. You get a great view from up top, correct?"

"Yes. It's definitely a selling point."

"So do you have to meet with anyone today?"

"I don't believe so." It's a quick ride to the tenth floor and as the doors open, I'm taken aback at the elegance. It's not what I would have expected for the rustic appeal of the rest of the hotel and resort. "This leads to my office and Daphne's, but down that way are the conference rooms."

"Good morning, Nancy," he says with a smile.

"Good morning, Mr. Turner." She has a smile on her face until she sees me and his hand in mine.

"Nancy, this is my fiancée, Maria."

"You're engaged?" she gasps, and I know immediately this woman is human and attracted to him. *Strange, I feel like I can smell her.*

So you can start to smell the way that we do now? Interesting. She's young and human, but not interested in me. It's the only reason I've allowed her to work so closely to my offices.

"It's nice to meet you, Nancy. I'll be doing my best to fill in for Daphne while she's out on maternity leave."

"It's a pleasure to have you here. If you need any help, please let me know." She picks up a stack of envelopes and hands them to Turner. "Here's the mail while you were out, sir."

"So I know you have a busy day ahead—can you point me to what you need me to do first?"

"Daphne's office is right here." He points to the door off to the right, but it's the door next to the large wall behind the receptionist that he pulls me into. "This is my office. Our office, to be exact." It's massive. Maybe the length of the wall and nearly just as deep. He has a large desk in the middle of the room where there is a view of the snowy mountain range behind him. Off to one side is a medium-sized round conference table and a sofa, and the walls are lined with bookshelves and cabinets.

"What's that door?"

"My private bathroom."

"That's awesome." I pause and then turn to face my mate. "So are we going to talk about what I need to do?"

"I see you're anxious to get to work."

"The sooner we get everything on track, the sooner we can relax together. I can sense your anxiety. What's it about? Your brother, the resort, us?"

"I can't help the worry when it comes to Max, but I believe it's everything. I've gone about our mating all wrong. I haven't told my people, but I suppose it doesn't really matter because I'm sure they'll all be coming to meet you one way or another. They're excited, from what I hear, but I'm feeling a little hesitant."

"Why, are you ashamed you—"

"Stop yourself right there. I'm not ashamed in the least. I don't want to share you with others. Human or shifter, I'm a crazy, jealous bastard and I'm not okay with it." I smile and wrap my arms around his waist and press my head against his chest.

"That's a much better answer."

There is a buzz on the intercom, so he reaches over and presses it. "Yes?"

"Mathias needs a word with you as soon as possible. There's a problem with a couple of servers."

"Okay. Is he on the phone, or did he come up here?"

"He's on the phone. Do you want to take it now?"

"I'll take it now. Please come in and show Maria

around Daphne's office and onto her computer."

"Yes, sir."

I kiss his cheek and then walk away. Turning back as I hold the door open, I wink and say, "Don't forget your call."

Closing it so he can have some privacy, I turn to Nancy, who's smiling at me nervously. It's not the kind of sketchy nervousness I've seen from people trying to hide something as a cop. It's probably because the pressure is on.

"So, how long have you been working for Turner?"

"I've been working for the company for five years, but I got bumped up here about a year ago, when the woman who had this position quit and moved out of the state. She didn't like the cold."

"Well, I'm relying on you to get me through my first day to help Turner. I'm sure you know some of the stuff Daphne does, but not all of it."

"Only a little. She's so dang efficient there's even an information folder for her temporary assistant. I've already taken care of the first two things on her list since they had to be done quickly and she was freaking out while going into labor."

"Well, that's crazy. Thank you for stepping up. Please, let's take a seat and go over this list. I'm not an assistant, I'm actually a Deputy for the Wolfe Creek police department. Well, I guess I was, so I know paperwork and I'm not afraid to talk to people, so that's all of my experience."

"That's pretty cool. It's amazing that you and the boss met and just hit things off and you left for him. I haven't met a man worthy enough to make me go out of my way for anything." She blushes because she's given me too much. People tend to do that, but that's why I made a great cop. A sadness washes over me as I think about not doing it anymore.

"Maria, can you come into my office, please?"

"In ten minutes. I need to learn some stuff."

Now. It's important.

"I need you to come in now."

"Coming." I stand up and say, "Excuse me." As soon as I'm in, his arms and his mouth crush down on me. "I'm sorry you're sad about having to leave your job for me."

"Damn, that mindreading shit sucks."

"Well, I think it's fantastic because I need to do all I can to make you happy."

"Is that what the rush in here was for?"

"No. I have to deal with some issues. I'll be back in about an hour or so, hopefully less."

"What's wrong?" Before he can say anything, I can hear his thoughts. Two females quit because they know we're together.

"Sorry. Damn it. I suppose this shit has a bad side."

"You know I can't do anything about them being upset and I sure as fuck didn't give them any attention, but now my restaurant manager's upset because they're short-staffed. I have to go put out those fires before things get worse."

"Where are those women?"

"They split. I'm guessing they expected to hook up with me, but you know how it works. I didn't notice them and only treated them like I do all my employees."

"Okay. I trust you, but just be careful. After what happened yesterday, I'm a bit afraid."

"I'll be fine. I promise. Now, I'll have some breakfast brought up in a bit."

"Egg and sausage wrap?"

"Yes. No cheese?"

"No, but would hash browns be too much?"

"Nothing is too much for you. Do you want them in the wrap or on the side?"

"Whatever works is fine with me. I'm hungrier than I thought I was."

"Maybe it's our little pup in there." He presses his hand to my stomach, and I sigh. It's way too soon to know, but the thought makes me happy. He spins me around and pats my ass. "Be good."

I go back into my office, and Nancy's on the phone at the desk. "Yes, actually. She's right here."

"Daphne would like to talk to you if you have a moment."

"Isn't she still in the hospital?"

She shrugs.

"Sure. Of course." She hands me the phone and then I cover it, letting Nancy know I'd like some privacy. I don't know what Daphne has to say, but it might not just be about the office.

Getting the hint, she walks to the door. "Okay. I'm going to my desk to see if I have any missed calls and voicemails."

"Thank you, Nancy."

I release my hand from the receiver and say, "Hello, Daphne. This is Maria."

"Hello, Maria. It's a pleasure to find out that Turner found you."

"Thank you. I've heard nothing but wonderful things about you from him. Congratulations on the new baby, although shouldn't you be resting in the hospital?"

"Thank you. I'm still in the hospital. I'm only calling to make sure you don't stress. Everything is under control, and most of his schedule is pretty straightforward."

"I'm looking at it now, but he's already had his day messed with. Two women from the restaurant just quit."

"Angel and Naevah?"

"I don't know their names. They were interested in Turner, but he's with me, and I guess that set them off and they left the restaurant manager in a bad place."

"Yep. It's those two. They're great at tips, but they weren't great with hiding their attraction to him. Sorry. He's a handsome man, and humans don't understand that he'd never pay them any mind. Of course, not you, but other humans."

"So you know?"

"I've done my research and know more about the Wolfe Creek pack, and so I learned that you worked for the Beta."

"Wow. You're a ball of information."

"That's my job." A little cry comes from over the phone. "Sorry, I have to go, but if you have any questions, Turner has my number."

"Thank you. Take care and rest up." I hang up, laughing to myself as I go over Turner's schedule. Daphne's one damn dedicated assistant. On the desk there's a notebook named "Notes" for my temporary replacement. I open it up and go to the page with all the temporary logins and sign into the computer.

I open up her emails and check for anything important while I wait for my breakfast to arrive. There's a new one from a linen company. I open it, and it says the next delivery is delayed a day. *Shit. Okay.* I read through the notes, and they need it for tomorrow. Luckily, I look at the date on the email and it was sent two days ago, so it should be arriving today instead of yesterday. I go through the emails, wondering why they were ordered so late and then I see there was a three-month delay on the materials.

The phone rings, and I pick it up without thinking it through. "Mr. Turner's office."

"Hey, beautiful. What's wrong?"

"Sorry. I just saw an email that said the towel delivery would be late."

"Yes. They just arrived. Luckily, this is only another order. We have plenty for the season, but backups are a must."

"Okay. I'm just getting the hang of things, so try not to freak out when you hear my mental concern. If I need you, I'll call for you."

"Fine. Just take it easy."

"Oh, speaking of relaxing, Daphne called me."

"Really?"

"Yes. She wanted to check on work and who had taken her place and since I was there, we chatted briefly. She knows I'm a human."

"I wouldn't put it past her. She's excellent for being

efficient and very stubborn in her pregnancy."

"I don't really mind at all. She told me if I needed anything to give her a call. She doesn't know how to rest."

"Nope, that's her. So I'm almost done with finding a few people to cover the shifts needed until I can hire more staff."

"Have you eaten?"

"I've picked at the food. How about you? Have you touched your food?"

"It hasn't arrived."

"What? It was sent up ten minutes ago."

"Oh goodness."

"Hold on." I hear him talking to someone away from the phone. *The wheel fell off the cart and the food toppled over. A broken serving cart. I'll bring you up a meal myself.*

"I'll be up there soon."

"Bye." I end the call and go back to working. It takes another ten minutes before Turner's back, and my stomach is rumbling wildly.

"I'm sorry, baby. I'm proving to be a terrible mate."

"It's okay. It's not a big deal."

"I could hear your stomach while I was still on the elevator."

"Are you serious?"

"No. I'm teasing, but I did hear it when I walked in. Here you go." He opens the lids on the tray and there's so much more than I originally asked for.

"I can't finish all of this. I hope some of it is for you."

"Yes, it is, but I want you to eat as much as you can. We have a busy day, and I still want to sink deep inside of you before bed."

"Then I better eat up." I giggle and then take a bite of my egg and sausage wrap. The hash browns are on the side, so I add some salt and pepper and go to town on the food. Turner's eating more than me, but he's nearly twice my size and could really use the extra calories, especially after the two days we've had together.

"Has it really only been two whole days?"

"Well, a little more than that, but we're getting closer to the three-day mark by this afternoon. It's the best three days of my life."

"I wouldn't say that. You got into a fight for me."

"No, it was because I pissed off an idiot and then you had to deal with it. You should be living the life of a queen."

"A queen is the right hand of her king. You're a busy man, and so that means you need someone to aid you, and that is me. I don't mind. It's been pretty easy this morning. Your assistant had everything ready to go. I've only had time to check emails. Your schedule's here, and it's already behind. You have a meeting with the housekeeping department and the ski instructors."

"You're starting to sound like Daphne, but eat first. I still have twenty minutes until the meeting with housekeeping. I have a dozen more cabins to inspect before the onslaught of guests in two days. Then, this place will be run like an efficient mad house." He smirks and shakes his head before devouring a slice of bacon.

"I'm starting to think you love bacon."

"Yep. I do, but I have something else I love to eat even more." He wags his brows, and he doesn't have to say anything for me to know. His thoughts are thoroughly fucked up, and my pussy throbs as I sit there attempting to not squirm in my seat.

"I'll behave. I want to get work done, and I don't have time to drill you before my meeting."

"Okay. Well, then, stuff your face and think clean thoughts, mister." I point my forkful of hash browns at him and he snatches it, wrapping his lips around the utensil and growling while he does it. Freaking jerk isn't helping me out.

"Now, you stop thinking dirty."

"I don't think these work breakfasts are going to be a thing. We'll never get anything done."

"I believe you have a point, but then that means I have to feed you before we leave the house."

I roll my eyes at him and then finish my wrap. I'm not full, but I don't want to be stuffed either, so I take one more bite of my potatoes and then set my fork down.

"Full?"

"Enough."

"Okay, do you want me to leave the fruit and juice with you so you can snack on it while I meet with the staff?"

"Sure. Thank you." He sets the carafe of orange juice and the fruit tray on the edge of my desk before placing a small kiss on my lips.

"Sorry, but I really do have to go." He walks away, and I feel the loss. I'm seriously pathetically obsessed with Turner, but I suppose that's natural.

My cell phone pings, and it's a text from Turner. **It's not pathetic. It's perfect because I'm obsessed with you.**

Stop being nosy.

Never. Now get your ass to work.

I would if my boss would stop harassing me.

Never.

Good.

A new email pings in, and it's a reporter wishing to interview Turner. I'll have to confer with him before I give a response. Given their secrets, I don't know if he does interviews at all. The rest of the morning passes in a hurry, and Nancy comes in around lunchtime. "I'm about to go to lunch. Here's a list of messages for the morning for Mr. Turner. Do you need anything from me before I go?"

"No. I didn't realize the calls were going to you."

"Normally they do when they're not in, but earlier Daphne called her direct line so it went straight through."

"Okay. Thank you, Nancy."

"Are you okay?"

"I'm fine. It's just a lot to learn in a short period of time. I know how important it is for him to have a great opening of the season."

"It will be alright. Everything's in order. They are never as busy as they usually are during these first weeks. Then, everything runs like clockwork. Here's my cell if you need to get a hold of me. And I've sent all calls to voicemail for now because you need time before you can start taking calls. All it's going to do is aggravate you."

"Thank you, Nancy. You're a treasure."

"Thank you," she says, grinning from ear to ear with the compliment. Do they praise her often? Maybe it's because they don't utilize her enough to show her skills, but she's been a great asset to me. She nods and then leaves the office, closing the door behind herself. I go over each message. Most of them are the businessmen trying to work with Turner. One is from the same news organization trying to get the scoop on Turner.

My cell phone rings, and it's Chloe. "Hey, Chloe, what's up?"

"Oh, Cat and I were just wondering if everything's okay."

"Everything's great now that I've met Turner."

"True. We just wanted to look after you. You've been great to us and the community, and now you're a sister of sorts to us."

"Thank you. Although our packs aren't related."

"Yes, but Cat and you were in the same boat. We think of you as family. I know Erik misses having your tough talk, tiny attitude around the station." I laugh because I'm a hard-ass always trying to be tough and Erik doesn't tolerate my need to overdo it.

"I miss him too." A snarl catches my attention. I look up at the door and say, "Ladies, I need to call you later."

"Turner, are you okay?"

"Who do you miss?"

"Oh, I was teasing. I haven't been gone long enough to really feel like I'm missing anyone. I was joking about Erik with Chloe and Cat."

"Oh," he sighs, ducking his head a little sheepishly. I almost feel bad for the jealous beast, but I'm sure he misses Daphne and I do my best not to be bothered by that, and they had a much closer relationship. They worked together daily, and she catered to his work needs.

"So what brings you here?"

"I saw Nancy going to lunch when I realized the time. I finished up with the instructors and then came straight up here."

"Are you hungry?"

"Not yet, but I have some paperwork and I thought I should check on you."

"That's so sweet of you." I test out my inner thoughts again. While stacking a bunch of papers, I think, *Damn, that tie is sexy.*

"I'm going to my office for the next hour. I'll order up some lunch and then you can take a short break with me before I have to start the inspections."

"Does Daphne usually do them with you?"

"Yes. She takes notes, but if you don't feel up to it, I can do it on my own."

"No. I can follow and jot down some notes for you. Besides, I want to see what the cabins look like. This is all new to me because other than the one stay we had at the hotel, I'd never been to one before. Even when I traveled up from El Paso, I had an apartment already set up in Seattle before I applied for the WCPD and then they gave me the apartment with Jacob."

"Well, then, it's best I show my queen around her territory."

"I can't wait."

"What do you want for lunch?"

"A small bowl of chili and crackers sounds so good to me."

"Great. I'll let them know. See you soon, love." His kiss is rough but I love it, so I let out a moan and then he quickly flies backward. "Okay. A bit too much." Turner squeezes his hard cock, then stomps out of the room like a spoiled child.

I love how put out he is about having to wait. I wonder if it will always be so passionate. Rubbing my fingers across my swollen lips, I can only hope so.

It's about half an hour after Turner left my office. I'm about to go check on him when the elevator door dings and then opens. I sense his presence even without having to see him. *I miss your thoughts this morning.*

Damn it. He's onto me. I start talking back. *I'm sorry, I've just been too focused on actual work.*

He walks into the room, and I breathe him in.

Marry me tomorrow.

"What?"

"You act like that's a bad thing?"

"Well, I do have a family back in Texas, so it kind of is."

"You know, if you're carrying my pup, they're going to be surprised by the sudden baby."

"Damn it."

"How about we get married next month? We'll start planning now."

"You forget I don't have the finances for the wedding."

"Are you kidding me, woman? What's mine is yours. I'll have a card expressed to you by tomorrow morning. Are there any more objections?"

"Why are you so anxious about it?"

"Because I want you to belong to me in every way."

"What brought this on, though? You were fine when

you left, and now you're freaking the fuck out about getting married."

"Someone said something that bothered me."

"What?"

"That men will see an engagement as not enough to stop flirting with you."

"Are you serious?" I stand up from around the desk and lock my office door. Then I cup my man's face and kiss him hard. A growl rips through him and he takes over devouring my mouth, kissing me as if it's for the last time. I pull back and then drop to my knees. "I'm yours in every way."

He moans as I run my hands up his thighs to his belt. He tips my chin up so that we're staring directly at each other. "And you're going to be a very good mate and suck my cock, aren't you?"

"Yes," I purr.

"Then take him out. Show me how much you need to please me." I slide his zipper down and pull his belt through the buckle, freeing it, and then unbutton my last obstacle. His cock pops free and I greedily suck the head, watching as his beast comes out. His eyes darken and his body stiffens as he fists my ponytail roughly. I pant and slide my tongue under his shaft while taking him all the way back until my nose brushes his short hairs. Fuck me, he pulls back and stares at me. "So unbelievably perfect. Suck, my queen." I moan around his length, reaching down with one hand on my breasts, rubbing them and slipping my other hand between my thighs, stroking my pussy through my pants. His need and mine race toward the finish as he fucks my face. How does this turn me into a mess? I'm a strong woman, but submissive to him in every way. He pulls completely out and then lifts me up, barely undoes the button on my pants while kissing me, and shucks them down before taking a seat on the sofa. He lifts me onto his length with my legs trapped by my pants, making it hotter that I'm held hostage by the material.

Come for me, Maria. Ride me. Fuck, just like that.

Yes, Alpha. Possess me. Our moans rip through the office, but it's our connection that screams it all. The sound of the lust in his voice drives my orgasm. I cry out his name as I come. "Josiah."

He covers my mouth with his. *You're mine. Your sounds are just for me.*

No one's here. Maybe just the receptionist. Let her hear, and then she'll know you belong to me.

She doesn't want me.

Blind man.

She doesn't flirt with me.

That's the only thing keeping me from slamming her head on the desk.

Bad girl.

He spanks my ass hard, thrusting upward until he roars out my name, coming deep inside of me.

I rest my head on his chest until we're both calm enough to move. We're a sticky mess, but I don't care. He helps me fix my pants and then fixes himself. When we step out, I blush because Nancy refuses to make eye contact with us. Good. She's lucky I need her assistance, but she's going to be moving to another department if she looks at Turner with that longing in her eyes again.

_____

8

Turner

WE LEAVE the offices for the day and head over to the hospital where Daphne and my cousin are with the newest addition to the pack. Maria picked up a pretty gift for Daphne and then one for the baby. When I arrive, I'm greeted by Daphne's mother and father. "Alpha Turner, Alpha Maria. It is an honor to have you visit."

"Thank you, but it's my honor. Daphne's not only a great assistant, but she's also family. Besides, I'm always thrilled to introduce my mate to everyone."

"How is the new family?" Maria asks.

"They are well. Visiting hours are nearly over, but I'm sure they won't have a problem." I look at the time on my watch. She's correct. It's nearly nine. We've been working hard and then had to stop and get a gift. We say our goodbyes and then head up to her room.

"Knock, knock," I say, pushing the door open just slightly

"Turner," Elijah calls out in a loud whisper. We enter and they both bow their heads lightly.

"Enough of that. How's the little one?" Elijah brings the bundle over to us. I take her in my arms and smile. She's adorable.

"I'd like you to meet the little princess, Ariel."

"Oh my! She's beautiful," Maria says, tears welling up in her eyes.

"Forgive me. Daphne, Elijah, it gives me great pleasure to introduce you to my mate, the lovely Maria."

"It's a pleasure to meet you, Alpha Maria."

"Yes, we already had our first conversation. I can say that you're one amazing woman. I don't know how I would have made it through the day without your many notes. We brought a little thing for the new mama and baby." I set the presents on the table next to the bed. "How long are you in here?"

"The labor was a little longer than expected, but we'll be going home in the morning. Your mother will be back to check on me."

"Great, so you'll be back just in time for the grand opening," I tease.

"Sorry, Alpha, but she's got to rest," Elijah says.

"I'm kidding, but knowing Daphne, she's anxious about tomorrow."

"You're right about that, but I'm sure you're in great hands."

"Yes, you've become my second favorite assistant."

"I'll take it. I'm so happy for you. At least that means you'll stop being a grumpy asshole."

"I couldn't help it. My wolf was restless." Maria plays with the baby's strawberry blonde hair, and I wonder if it'll darken like Daphne's or lighten like Elijah's.

"Can I hold her?"

"Of course." I hand the little baby girl to Maria.

"You're good with babies," Maria says.

"I've been around for a lot of new babies. Pack members are happy to show me their babies. Trust me when I say you'll get all the cuddle time you could ever want, love."

"I don't think I'll ever get enough. I have a lot of nieces and nephews, and this never gets old."

The baby starts to let us know that she's hungry by hunting for Maria's chest. "Hey, that's mine."

Laughing, Maria hands the baby back to Daphne. "He's a bit possessive."

"Just a bit," Daphne teases.

"We'll leave you to it. Take it easy. I mean it. The both of you. I don't expect to see you around for a while, unless we come to visit. Understood?"

"Yes, Turner."

We take our leave and I bring Maria's hand up to my lips, kissing it as we wait for the elevator. "I dread and welcome the day you bring our little one into the world."

"Dread?"

"I never want you to suffer, my love."

"Thank you for finding me." We share a brief kiss before the elevator opens up to the lobby. We walk out, smiling, knowing the best is yet to come.

*I*t's opening day and the guests are piling in, the restaurant is set up, and my mate is looking beautiful in a pair of snow pants and a coat. We're going around welcoming guests and checking with the instructors who are already taking their first students.

"How are you holding up?" I ask Maria, sliding up beside her with my hand around her waist.

"I'm doing very well. It's hectic, but I'm finding it entertaining."

"Okay. Well, do you think you could work for the resort from now on?"

"What about Daphne?"

"Oh, I didn't mean as my assistant. I don't want you working that hard."

"What am I supposed to do?"

"I don't know, baby. What do you want to do?"

"Do I have to decide now? Isn't it going to be several weeks before Daphne returns?"

"You have plenty of time to decide. Have you called your parents yet?"

"I haven't."

"What are you waiting for?"

"They're going to ask a thousand questions, and I'm not sure that I have all the right answers."

"I suppose you do have a point. It's not like your family would understand, but they don't need to know that we've only just met. You can tell them that we've been dating for months and that we're not rushing as fast as they believe."

"That could work. What about the..."

"Excuse me, sir. I didn't mean to interrupt, but the chief of police is here. He wants a word with you."

"Sure. I'll be down there in a few minutes."

"The chief of police?"

"Yes. He's probably just checking on the arrivals. It's extremely busy, and his men have to double down on the patrols."

"Okay. I understand. I'll go with you. I want to meet the chief you mentioned before."

We make our way down to the entrance of the main hotel where there sits a pudgy man in a police uniform with a bulky coat, useless when you have to apprehend a perp on the run. I already get a sense that he doesn't care about his job.

"So who do we have here?" he questions with a little more interest than acceptable. I hold back my revulsion, making sure to keep my thoughts popping out every few minutes so Turner doesn't know that I'm practicing blocking him out.

"She's not for you to be staring at, Chief Anderson. Maria, the chief of police in White Wolf Ridge. Chief, my fiancée, Maria."

"Fiancée? That's quick. No one knew you were dating. That seems to happen a lot around here. Everyone gets together without much fanfare." There's too much suspicion in his question that has the hairs on the back of my neck standing up.

"And your point?"

"Nothing. I'm simply curious."

I don't like his suspicions.

Me either. That's another reason why I want to get rid of him.

"So what can we help you with, Chief?" *And he appears lazy.*

"You know. I just came to warn you to keep us abreast of any incidents. I know the mayor's your father, but there's still law and order around here. I learned about the fight you covered up for your brother."

"A little rough-housing between young men, and neither of them were really hurt. It's nothing to press charges for."

"It's still an incident."

"So some paperwork for you to fill out for nothing." *What a prick!*

"Thank you for your reprimand, Chief. We have to keep everything in order before chaos ensues, but if there is an issue with the guests or staff, we'll contact the station. Then you can send someone prepared to make an arrest."

"I'll be quick to be here." *Quick? My ass.*

What a very nice ass. "Very well. Filling in as his temporary assistant, I have to keep Mr. Turner on track. Excuse us."

Always thinking about my body. What am I going to do with you?

Submit to my desires.

I barely let the men shake hands and then I hook my arm in the crook of Turner's and spin us around, walking without another word to Anderson.

"Wow. That was good," I grunt. My mate's a tough woman.

"I've dealt with many overinflated egos before. Some men put on a badge just to make up for their lack of manliness. It just rolls off him."

"You're talented, although I'd love to meet all the egos that insulted you."

"I don't think you want to, or you'd have a trail of dead bodies."

"I'd do anything for you, Maria."

"I know, and that's enough for now." Her cell rings in her pocket, so she checks who's calling but sends it to voicemail. I don't like that shit. I trust her, but if she's having a problem with someone, I want to be the one to deal with it.

"Who was that?"

"My dad," she sighs.

"Why didn't you answer it?" I already know the answer to that and say it. "Are you afraid of telling them the semi-truth?"

"Yes. I'm sorry. I will do it after we call it a day at work. As soon as I figure out what to tell them."

"I can handle it, but I know you want to do it, and I'm going to hold you to it."

"Shit," I grumble. Now it's my phone going off. I pull it out and see that there's a problem at the front desk. "Okay. Someone wants to speak to the manager."

"I'm with you." We walk to the front, and I keep my hands on my phone and not on my mate. It's hard to avoid touching her, but I already have a disgruntled guest. We arrive up front to see a man I recognize immediately.

"Is there something I can help you with, Mayor

Turner?" I ask, hoping it's nothing serious because today's been good so far despite all the hiccups leading to today.

"Well, hello, my darling Maria. It's good to see you. And yes. Your mother is upset that you two have been dragging on marriage planning, and she sent me here to harass you."

"Is that really why you're here?" I have a sinking suspicion it's not.

"Okay. I just wanted to see if you heard from your brother."

"I haven't spoken to him in two days. Why? What's wrong?"

"He got into trouble in Lakeland, Florida. I'm on my way there. I wanted you to keep an eye on your sister. Your mother insists she come with me so we can talk to your brother together."

"Of course, I'll look after Aria. She can stay with us. I hope everything's okay."

"You know that Anderson came from Lakeland," he adds pointedly. I know damn well what he means.

"Are you serious?" Does Anderson have anything to do with my brother getting into some shit, or has his hot head gotten the better of him? Damn it. I hope he's okay.

"Yes. I have a feeling he has a hand in whatever happened with your brother."

"I'll bury that bastard if he does."

"I'm with you on that, son."

"He was just here, reminding me that he's in charge of the law, not me."

"Do you think he knows?"

"No, he mentioned the fight Max got into with the guy from Wolfe Creek, which I wasn't aware he knew about since we kept it a pack matter."

"The bastard. When I come back, he's out, but in the meantime, stay out of his way. I don't want the fucker trying to arrest you for something. If he really becomes a problem, we'll have to deal with him the old way." I know exactly what he means and without a doubt, we'll rip him limb from limb.

Maria gasps.

It's the nature of the beast.

Oh, that's not it. He must know about you all.

Do you really believe that?

Yes. Too many questions about the quick relationships, and now this. Someone needs to sneak into his home and find out all they can on him.

"Care to share with the class?" my father asks, guessing from our silence that we're having a private conversation.

"We can talk when you get back. Be careful, and let me know what's going on as soon as you can and if you need anything."

"Okay. You two be careful and keep your guard up. We don't need a repeat of what happened in Wolfe Creek." We both nod, and then he pulls us in for a hug. I turn and see Anderson watching us.

"The bastard's still here," I mutter in a hush that only they can hear.

"Calm down, my love. Let's get to work." Her soft hand on my forearm does the trick again.

"Be safe, Father. We must get back to resort duties."

"See you soon." He walks off right past the chief without a word or any acknowledgement of the man.

9

Maria

TURNER and I walk away without addressing the chief again because it won't end well, so we pivot toward the bank of elevators. I know where my mate needs to go, and that's to his office so he can get out some of the tension that has brought his wolf toward the surface. I can sense it, feel it as if it's me with such Alpha energy ready to strike.

The second the elevator doors close around us, he locks it down from inside. Turner has me in his arms, crushing his mouth to mine, pinning me to the wall of the elevator. There are no cameras in this elevator because it's his private one and only the three people on the floor can access it. He grabs the clasp on my dress pants and undoes it, pulling down my pants and panties before spinning me around to face the wall. In seconds, I feel the cool air hit my ass before his hand comes down and then he slams inside of me with a grunt. His fingers lace with mine as he presses them up above my head on the wall. Fucking me with only his strong thighs driving his cock deep inside me, I cry out, feeling every inch of my mate. His pleasure is mine, and I swallow my screams so only he can hear them in my head. Listening and feeling my release, he lets go as well, emptying himself in me.

We're both panting wildly as he presses his body on mine. "I could live like this."

"Me too. I thought we'd make it to the office, but I underestimated you." I moan, shaking my ass while he's still buried inside of me. I start him up all over again, and it's another twenty minutes before we make it to his office.

Three hours later, we're walking into our home. Before I get to start dinner, Turner pulls me in for a kiss and says, "Make the call."

"Fine."

I drop down on the sofa. "I'll start dinner." He kisses my cheek and walks away. I know he'll be able to hear my thoughts and the call, so he'll be here in a heartbeat if I need him, but I'm still nervous.

I check my call log and hit the missed call from my dad, then press the call icon while releasing a harsh sigh.

"Ah, I love that sigh. It's good to hear. I was quite worried about you, mija."

"I'm fine, Papa. Donde esta, Mama?"

"Aqui," she says, right next to the phone.

"Bueno. Voy a casar en un mes," I blurt out and wait.

"Que dice? Quien? Who?"

"My fiancé."

"Y su prometido es?" my mother asks in frustration.

"His name is Josiah Turner."

"Híjole, un guero. Yo se, yo se. You thought we would care that he's not Mexican, no? But we don't care as long as he's not a pinche cabrón. Quiero hablar con el," my father says.

"Right now?"

"Si."

"Turner, my dad wants to talk to you," I say as Turner shows up, rubbing my back. I know he can hear the whole conversation without having it on speakerphone.

"Hello, Senor Arroyo. I'm Josiah Turner, and I'm in love with your daughter."

"That is good, but what are your intentions?"

"My intentions are to live a full and happy life with your daughter at my side until my dying days."

"How are you to take care of my daughter? Provide for her?"

"First, she will always be treated as a queen in my eyes, but as a police officer, she has shown that she is more than capable of caring for herself. I understand what you mean, though, and I own the resort in White Wolf Ridge. As my assistant is out on maternity leave, Maria has been wonderful filling in."

"Maternity leave? Who is..." I know where he's going, and Turner's getting riled up really fast. My father's just being a father, but I'm sure Turner doesn't care.

"Mr. Arroyo, I will stop you right there. I fired a stupid kid for making a comment implying that same thing. That is a disrespect on me and on my cousin's wife."

"Forgive me, but we have known that it is common."

"Not in my world, it isn't." I brush his arm and nuzzle his neck because I know he's offended and I need him to calm down.

"I apologize, but I must look out for my daughter's best interest. She may be an adult, but she will always be my daughter."

He tightens his hold on me, rubbing his hard cock on my ass, and I have to hold back a moan. "I understand. Maria's my priority and always will be, and nothing will happen to her. I will protect her with my life and give her my soul."

"That's good to hear, but only time will tell. So what's the urgency?" he asks as Turner slides his tongue over the tops of my breast.

"Because I have to let everyone know that she's mine, and she feels the same."

"That's for sure," I offer, holding back the whimper that comes from me.

"We will be handling everything from here. I'm sure Maria's going to want to plan with her mom, but I'll leave that to her. I'll send my private jet to pick up whoever's coming."

"A private jet? So you're wealthy?"

"Yes, but that has no bearing on our relationship."

"Yes, but it does make me feel a little more confident that you can truly care for her financially, especially if you start having children."

"Good. As long as we understand each other." His phone rings in his pocket, vibrating on my ass, so he lifts me up to get it. I can see it's Mark, so I slide off him.

"Excuse me, but I have a call that I have to take. It was great talking to you."

He stands up, giving me an apologetic frown before handing the phone back while walking away in a hurry. I sense his tension, and then it's gone.

Bastard. He's learned to shut me out.

"Mama, Papa, sorry, but he has a work call. Someone always needs something," I say.

"So about the wedding. Let's talk about who's coming and the exact date." My mother goes over the list, and that's just too much for me. I don't want my entire extended family there. A courthouse wedding is looking better and better every single day.

If that's what you want, my love.

Listening in now?

Always.

But keeping me out.

Just waiting until you're done talking to your parents. Then we can talk.

Okay.

"Mom, I have to go finish dinner. I'll talk to you later."

"Okay. Call me tomorrow."

"It will have to wait until we finish work. I'm helping him out, and it's crazy how much goes on in a day," I explain.

"That's fine. I'll be at the shop until six anyway." My parents own a local grocery store, so they understand how busy life is.

I end the call and go straight to Turner's office, where he's pacing. "What's wrong?"

"Mark says that Anderson has been scoping out my assistant's house and saw my cousin shift."

"Shit. So what's going to happen?"

"I don't know, but the first thing is to catch him off guard where he doesn't have a weapon. I don't want to kill him, but I will be put in that position. I can't have him exposing us as well as trying to kill my people."

"You have to do what you have to," I say.

"I want you to stay here. My sister's already being brought here by Mark. Then we're going to meet before we decide what to do."

"I don't like this."

"Me either, but I can't let anything happen to you. We're going to be okay."

"You don't know that. Look at what happened to you at the other resort. We're in this together."

"We already have men on the ground watching his every move, and that's the reason he was caught. We've cut the signal to his phone and the dispatcher cut his radio. There's nowhere for him to go but home. I just want to talk to the bastard, but I won't be alone."

"Okay, but if something happens to you, I'm going to kick everyone's ass."

"Fine. Just so you know, today you will become chief. I'm not going to let anyone step up into the position that isn't one of us. Are you ready to lead?"

"Are you serious? You're trusting me with that duty?"

"I'd trust you with my life. You already have the experience to do it. The only reason you weren't promoted in Wolfe Creek was your human status. Now you're one of us, even if you haven't shifted yet."

"I know I can do it, but I didn't think you wanted me to be in law enforcement," I remind him.

He cups my face and kisses my nose. "I don't want you patrolling, but I'm not against you sitting behind the desk, giving orders and delegating." He gives me a smile.

"I can manage that, and I won't be a total lazy prick."

"Good. So let me handle this, and then I turn over the station to you."

"Fine, just come back to me. That matters more than anything else." I can't lose him.

"I will. You're my priority, but I am still the pack Alpha."

"I know. Kiss me before you go."

"Always." His mouth crashes down on mine. His kiss is hard, dominating as he swipes his tongue along mine. I thrust my hands into his hair, bringing us closer. I need more, and he delivers.

The sound of the car pulling up in the driveway pulls us apart. "Mark's here."

"Sorry, love." He kisses the top of my head. I smile up at him before walking to the front door. Aria comes running up the stairs and throws her arms around me.

"Maria, it's a girls' night!"

I love his little sister. She's exuberant and sweet. The men share a look of concern on their faces, so I take Aria in the house because they've business to discuss. I understand that there are levels of authority. Turner is still my mate and we are close to equals, but I'm not strong yet and I'm a liability to them. If I ever shift, then I'll be able to give him a little help. Even then, I doubt he'd ever want me involved.

"So you need to tell me more about Jacob. I know you lived with him, so you must know what he likes and what he doesn't?"

"You don't even know if you're mated to him yet, but if it makes you feel better, I'll give you a little bit about him. You know what he looks like, but you haven't had time to spend with him. He's more than his good looks. He's really smart, like book smart. He works for the Wolfe Creek Police department now. He only started after graduating from college. He loves the outdoors, which I'm starting to suspect is what most shifter men enjoy."

"Yes, and most of the women too. I think it's the wolf in us. Speaking of, we have to figure out how to get you to shift."

That's something that bothers me. I have no idea when or if I will ever shift, and it might take a serious injury to Turner. I'd rather never shift than for that to happen.

We work on dinner to keep our minds off of what the guys are up to. We're about to eat when the sound of a car comes up the driveway. It doesn't sound like Turner's or Mark's vehicle, but then I look, and it's Nancy with a file folder.

"Shit. Act cool. She's the receptionist for Turner."

"Oh, yeah. I recognize her."

"Hey, Nancy," I greet her on the porch. Fuck, I should have put on a coat.

"I brought some papers that need to be signed for Mr. Turner," she says, holding her large purse.

"He's out with the guys. Poker night," Aria says. "You can drop them off. I'm sorry you came all this way."

"No. That's okay. Can I use the little girls' room, though? The cold air hit me, and now I have to go."

"Sure." We let her in, and she goes straight to the bathroom like she's been here before. If I didn't know better, I'd be jealous.

"Has she been here before?"

"Not that I'm aware of, but maybe she pulled the same thing with him before."

"I bet," I scoff. I can't believe Turner never noticed her interest. Then again, he's a guy—a dense shifter who wouldn't know that she was being more than sweet.

Still, I try to keep my cool because she can't take my man from me. I just want her ass out of my house. She comes out a minute later, and then that's when I see a different look in her eyes. It's not sweet, nice, or even envious. She's on drugs. Did she do a line or something like that?

"Are you okay, Nancy?"

"I'm fine."

"So the papers?" I ask.

"I'll just wait to give them to the boss."

"You can leave them with me."

"No, I can't, because you forgot them in the first place. You'll probably be too busy gagging on his cock to remember to do your job. At least Daphne could control herself around the boss. You seduced him, and that's why he gave you the spot. He's just like every other man."

"Excuse me?"

"Don't act all innocent. I had a camera put in there to watch Daphne and him to see if she was having an affair, but they never did anything. You, on the other hand, were a dirty little whore with my man. I thought he would notice me, and then I just assumed he was gay, but then you came in and let him fuck you. I suppose he has a thing for Latinas."

"My brother loves Maria. What they do is their business, and you're going to regret everything you've said here." Aria moves to get in front of me, but that's when Nancy pulls a gun. Shit. I don't have my service revolver anymore.

"I'll kill you both before I let you steal my life." The shot goes off before I know what happens, but Aria's mid-shift, then she's hit with a bullet. I scream out.

"Bitch, you see I'm serious."

"You don't have to do this."

"Too late." I don't know who says that, whether it's me or her, but I don't think...I just react. The shot goes off, but all I see is my mate in my head.

10

Turner

"Where is Merrick?" I ask Mark as we get to my SUV. It's faster, and I can reach anyone from it.

"He's parked outside Anderson's residence. They're waiting for you to move on the situation."

"Let's go, then."

"Aren't you going to say bye to your mate?"

I love you. Be strong, my queen.

I love you, too. Stay powerful, my warrior.

"Done. Now let's go. We don't have much time to waste."

"That's a pretty cool thing." He shakes his head and smiles.

"It is, but we don't have much time. I want him to be caught off guard. How many weapons does he have in his house?"

"An arsenal."

"Damn it. Fine." We're only about fifteen minutes

from his residence. It's pissing me off that he played this game. What's his goal? Thinking about my plan, I say, "I want to talk."

"We can open a line and call him. What are you thinking?"

"Maybe the bastard is just curious. Maybe he doesn't mean any harm and witnessed all the sudden marriages and babies. Maybe Hunter was right to keep humans out of the area as much as possible. We've welcomed them into our midst, and now we're at risk of exposure."

"Yes, but as you say that, you've mated with a human," he reminds me.

"I know, but apparently it's only the Alphas that are mating with humans. I'm not saying we get rid of them or anything. I'm just saying we need to be a fuckload more careful." I can't lose Maria. Never. I'll do whatever I have to, even if it means closing the resort, keeping the shifters to one side of the town. Something has to give.

"Well, that's the problem. No one expects to be spied on in their home," he says. He has a point. Whether or not we live next door to them, if they spy on us, they'll learn more than we want them to know about us. I'm shaking with rage just thinking about Anderson stalking Daphne and Elijah, but I'll pay the bastard back.

"True. Now let's turn the tables," I add.

We pull up and Merrick is sitting in his car, watching and listening from a distance.

"What's going on inside there?" I ask in a whisper.

"He's checking his weapons. I don't know what he has planned, but he's alone in there."

"Okay."

"Open the line," I tell Mark. He hands me a dummy phone and presses the call button. He doesn't answer the first time. In fact, he stares at his phone in awe and suspicion. With the blessing of keen sight at night, we can see right through his basement window, even though he has most of it blocked off. He's waiting for a war. Nut case.

"Do I continue to call?"

"Yes."

On the second call, he picks up on the last ring. "It seems you've been a Peeping Tom, which is illegal as fuck. Something I wouldn't expect from a man of the badge."

"Turner, call your dogs off."

"What dogs? I haven't done anything. You, on the other hand, have committed several offenses. Tsk, tsk."

"What are you going to do?"

"Nothing. I'm just curious as to what you're going to do?"

"A good dog is a dead dog."

"Don't make it come to that. I assure you that it won't end well for you."

"No, maybe not, but I'll be taking that bitch of yours with me to the other side."

"What?"

"You won't make it out of the building."

"I don't have to. My work is already being done for me. I knew you'd want to keep her safe."

"Bullshit."

"You'd be surprised what people are willing to do when they believe they can get super powers too."

Maria, tell me you're okay.

Someone's here.

Get into the basement safe room. Take my sister. I love you. I'm on my way now.

No!

"Make it look like we're all leaving. Get him when he thinks he's safe. Tie him up, and I'll deal with him."

I jump into my truck with Mark, and Merrick jumps into his. We race down the road. I know Merrick's going to sneak out and hide, but I have to get to my mate.

"Call Maria." My truck rings, but she doesn't answer.

I'm coming, my queen. Suddenly I feel an intense pain, and then it eases.

"Fuck, she's not answering me."

We pull up to the house in less than eight minutes, and there's a minivan parked next to Mark's truck.

We step out, and he slices the tires as he passes. I step in and watch the scene in front of me. My sister's on the floor, but then my mate snarls and growls, pouncing on Nancy who has a gun in her hands. The gun flies out and Maria bites Nancy's jugular, ending the young woman. God, my wife is gorgeous in her white fur and honey eyes. I run in and make sure Nancy's dead before I rub my mate's head. "I love you." She relaxes and shifts effortlessly back into human form as if she's done it a thousand times. Swiftly, I grab the throw off our sofa and toss it on Maria. Then I hear a groan.

"Aria!"

Maria and I hurry to my sister, and Mark is pressing his shirt to her shoulder. "We need to get her to a hospital."

"I'm fine. God, Maria's a badass Alpha female."

"I want to be badass like that one day."

"That she is."

"Mark, can you drive her to the hospital?"

"I can."

"I'm going to help Maria wash up and deal with this, and then I'll be at the hospital in an hour."

"Don't worry about me." She winks. My sister's more badass than she knows.

"Mate, stay here while I get rid of this one here." I grab the body and run through the woods to where I know a small pack of mountain lions live. I toss the body in there, and it's not more than a minute before they're devouring what is left of Nancy. She shouldn't have come after my mate. This is for the best.

I rush back to the house to see the blood on the floor has already been cleaned up and the shower's running. Leaning up against the wall, my mate sobs hard. I grab a towel and pull my woman out, turning off the water before carrying her to our bed. With her in my lap, I let her cry.

"Oh my goodness, we have to go." She flies off me, the towel falling. "We promised Aria." Damn it, I'm not supposed to be so damn horny right now.

"Yes, get dressed." I still have another bastard to deal with. I close my eyes and think about the shit I have to do. I strip and shower because I have some of Nancy's blood on me. After a quick wash, I meet my mate downstairs.

"I'm sorry you had to kill her."

"It's not that I had to kill her. I'm upset about it, but it's more about your sister getting hurt. How can I be your mate if I can't protect her?"

"Or how can I be your mate when I couldn't protect you?"

"That's not true. You had no idea."

"Yes, and Nancy has been nothing but nice to you until now, so how could you have known? How could we have known?"

"She was obsessed with you. She wanted you to marry her. She heard us having sex in Daphne's office."

"Oh shit. Yes, she forgot something and came back. She was angry and then saw the chief." Fuck, what makes me so damn appealing to the opposite sex? It's insane.

"I'm so sorry, my love." I say as I slip on my jeans. Maria watches with admiration. "We'll make up for lost hours tonight. I'm still going to have to call my parents about this."

We get in my truck, and I call Mark. "She's getting stitched up. She's good. It was a through and through. The doc gave her a meds script that I'll put in for you."

"We're on our way now."

"Okay. See you soon. We won't leave until you get here."

"I have to call my parents."

My dad picks up on the first ring. "Please tell me everything's okay."

"It will be soon. We have a serious problem." I explain what happened, and he says, "Save that bastard for me. He could have killed both my babies."

"He wouldn't have gotten the drop on me. I was careless with my mate."

"No. You did the right thing, and if your mate had

died, you would have died. You know that as much as I do."

"True. I don't want to even consider that."

"I know. I'm sure you don't."

"What happened with Max?"

"Nothing. The bastards put him in jail for supposedly committing a homicide, but after records showed he'd just arrived in town, he was cleared. It made no sense, and I know it all has to do with that asshole chief. He wanted me out of town so you'd have less reinforcements."

"I know. I'm glad, though, that you're all safe."

"We're almost at the hospital to pick up Aria."

"I need to talk to my daughter."

"Call Mark. He's waiting there with her."

"Okay." We end the call, and I squeeze Maria's hand and bring it to my lips.

"Your wolf is beautiful, Maria. Just so you know. It's fucking sexy as hell."

"Sexy?"

"Yes. You pounced before she could figure out what was happening, and then you shifted back into your sexy human form like it's natural to you, proving that you were meant for me."

"Stop saying things like that. We have to get your sister, and now I'm horny."

"I know. I can feel your pussy fluttering without even having to have my fingers sliding through your plump little lips." Before she could say something with venom, we pull into the hospital parking lot.

We're in the foyer when Aria pushes herself up out of the wheelchair. "I told them I don't need it."

I looked at the doctor who we all know because he's one of our own. "Thank you," I say.

"Just doing my job, Alpha," he whispers that last bit. "Excuse me, but I have another patient coming in. Apparently there was someone shooting off guns like an idiot in the woods. Drunk teens not realizing what goes up must come down." He shakes his head and walks away.

"Ready to go?"

"Yes. We never got to finish our ice cream, and I'm super hungry all of a sudden." Ten minutes later, she's asleep in the back seat.

"She's exhausted. It's been a day from hell, hasn't it?"

"That's for sure. I'm tired too."

"I bet. It takes a while to get used to shifting. When we're pups and first start shifting, we sleep a lot more."

"I'll take you both up to bed, and then we can get this all squared away." Maria walks alongside me while I carry my sister into the house. As soon as I have my sister in her temporary room here, I scoop up my tired mate and take her to our room. Once I tuck her in, I give her a deep kiss. "I have a few things to deal with, but I'm not leaving this time. I'll be downstairs and up to bed as soon as everything is settled."

As soon as I'm downstairs, Mark, Merrick, and Elliot are on my steps. "So what's going on, guys?"

"It's too late. His house blew up. I don't know if he accidentally set off the explosion, but we won't know anything until the fire department is done."

"I'm about to go there now and investigate," Elliot says. He's the chief of the fire department and the fire investigator.

"Good. Let us know what you find. I need to know if he's dead or not."

"Of course." He nods and walks out of the house to his fire chief SUV.

"So what happened to the dumb bitch?"

"She's food for the mountain lions."

"Good. Should we put her vehicle on the road near the mountain pass without any gas?"

"Sounds good. Siphon every drop out, so it looks like she stopped there and got lost. She was a hiker, so maybe she thought she could walk back and met with foul play. It's snowing now. Any prints will be covered by morning."

I smile. "It's very true. I did make sure to drag her with blood dripping just in case." The animals would have dragged her to a secluded spot.

"Great. Now let me get inside to the new chief of police."

"Your mate?" I nod. "Awesome. It fits." We shake goodbye, and the guys get to work.

Nothing can be done until morning, so I lock up and head to our room. After stripping down to my boxers, I put on some pajama pants just in case my sister wakes up. Maria rolls into my arms and snuggles down with me. It feels so damn good to get some sleep.

The sun is starting to rise when I hear my sister groan. I get up and go to her room. "How are you feeling?"

"Like shit, but I'm sure it will pass. How's Maria?"

"She's still sleeping. Yesterday was pretty damn insane."

"For sure." The doorbell rings.

"Stay put." I get up and head down. I can smell my parents outside, so I open the door and Max is with them. They all rush in, hugging me.

"Where's my baby?"

"In bed. You got here fast."

"We flew out as soon as we got off the phone with Aria. Florida's too damn hot for us."

"What about you, bro?"

"Same. I can't leave you on your own without shit going wrong."

"Right."

Aria walks down the stairs holding onto Maria.

"So I heard you're a full shifter too. Thank you," Max says, pulling Maria in for a hug. I hold back my growl and snarl. I know they need to bond.

"I'm hungry. Turner's trying to starve me. I didn't even get any red meat last night. Maria's greedy." She winks. I roll my eyes.

"How about some coffee and some breakfast?"

"Yes. I need some coffee. Shit. We need to get to the resort. I've already cancelled any meetings, but we can leave at ten. It's fine. Everything's running smoothly."

"I'm sure it is."

My cell rings, and it's Elliot. "He's not in there. There's a body, but it's not his. Even with the charred flesh, I know he had a replacement inside."

"In case his plans went awry. I'm on my way to the hotel in a bit. Where the hell could he go? It's not like he can explain why there's a dead body in his basement."

"I'm going to have to cut breakfast short. I'll take some toast and a coffee to go."

"It's fine. We can eat at the hotel."

"You should stay here."

"Did that work so well last time?"

"No, but my brother and father weren't here. I don't trust Anderson. He's a sneaky fuckhead. He's got to be coming after me." I kiss my mate hard as hell. "Protect her with your life. I'm going to find this asshole and shoot him myself."

"We will."

I close my eyes and walk away before I take her with me. I rush into the garage, pulling out some hunting guns, and then open my trunk, staring at the CPR dummy in the back of my truck that will come in handy. I'm glad I didn't drop it off. Running back into our bedroom, I pull out some of Maria's clothes and a winter hat, and then I run out the back.

Once I pull out with the fake Maria, a bad feeling rolls up my spine. I hate the idea that someone could come after her, but I still drive onto the main road. I'm only a quarter mile from the house when a shot rings out. My truck window shatters, and I feel the dummy fall onto my shoulder. I pull over, and another shot rings out. I can hear it as clear as day and know the direction it came from.

I'm out of my vehicle after nudging the dummy off me. Rage soars through my bones, and my wolf feels the anger. If that had been my mate, she would have been dead. There are no words that will ever suffice to say how violent I feel. I shoot in the direction of the shot as I run for cover behind a large tree. Another shot rings out. My ears are perked up, listening to target my next shot. Smiling, I take the shot, seeing the top of that fuck's head. I scalp the fucker and he falls hard, rolling down the hill. Sirens are going off, and it's Officer Holden, who is a shifter as well. He jumps out with his gun.

"It's me, Holden," I call out.

"I see your vehicle." He sees the body of the former chief on the slope, body slumped around a tree.

"What the fuck? He's supposed to be dead at his house."

"I'm guessing the corpse you found is a decoy. That fucker came after my family last night, and I think he used the fire as a diversion to come after me."

"I see. Shit. This is fucked up. I heard he found out about us."

"Yes. Only some. Since you're not mated, I don't think he knew you were one."

"Are you okay?"

"Yes. I'm not injured. Just a little broken glass, but he was aiming for my mate—or who he thought was my mate."

"Let me get the coroner over here. Luckily most of those in charge are shifters like us. There won't be too many questions. Fucking humans can't leave us alone." I raise my brow. "Sorry. I didn't mean your mate. It's just people like him and the women and men who flirt with us. It's as if they find us even more appealing than they should."

"You're right about that. It's nuts."

"Well, I'll need to take your statement officially, just in case. I'm sorry, but you're going to have to stay here for a bit."

"No problem, but I need to make a call." I create some distance and then call my wife who's frantic.

"I'm safe, but I need to talk to the police. Tomorrow you come in to talk to your new team. I love you. I'll be home in an hour. I'm going to do my best to handle business from home today."

"Are we safe now?"

"Yes. The threat has been eliminated, but I can't guarantee if there's any more. He blew up his house with all the physical evidence."

"We'll have to do a sweep of his tech."

"Yes, ma'am." I end the call and talk to Holden, who writes everything down. We're almost done when the coroner arrives.

"This bastard? I have a dead body in my morgue that I was to believe was him."

"Well, unless he has a twin, this asshole wanted me dead for the firing my father was in the process of handling when he was taken away with a family emergency."

"I understand. Is this your truck?" He walks over to it. "Get photos," he tells the crime scene tech that just arrived. "Fuck me. If this had been Maria…"

"I know. I had a sick feeling and thought it was a smart idea. Now I'm fucking sick to my stomach."

"It was for the best. If he didn't target her, you would

have been the target. You're smart for leaving her elsewhere, but is she safe there too?"

"Yes, my dad and brother are back and watching over her."

"Good. Damn, they've put a lot on your plate since you've become Alpha."

"I hope it's over. I have a mate to spend my life with and a bunch of pups to make."

"Your vehicle is going to need a new wheel too."

"Along with a fuckton of body work. Do you want me to call in a tow?"

"Yeah, I don't want Maria to see this."

"Good. Do you need a ride back home?"

"No. I'll just walk. I need the air right now."

"Take it easy."

"It's about a five-minute walk." I shake their hands and take my two unused guns with me and leave the one I used with them for any forensics they might need. The cold mountain air feels good in my lungs as I breathe in the chaos today. This has to be one of the most violent and intense weeks ever, and I hope to never have this experience again.

I step onto my property, and I barely get halfway to the house when Maria comes out running with a nervous smile on her face. She's in my arms, legs wrapped around my waist and lips on mine. "You're alive. I felt the tension, and we could hear the shots from here. They wanted to leave, but they couldn't leave us unprotected."

"That's very smart of them. We'll need a new truck, but I'm fine. And if you don't stop rubbing up on me, I'm going to take you on the fucking steps."

"I believe that's our cue to leave," my father says.

"No, please stay for the time being. I know you'll have to make a statement. The press will be here soon, and there's no true way to spin the story."

"Good. Well, then, you're just in time for breakfast. I was so nervous, I just kept cooking."

"Don't go upsetting your mother, or we'll be having a feast all the time."

"Wait, maybe you should. I'm a growing young man," my brother says, snatching a piece of bacon off the plate. I snarl and grab one for myself.

We spend the rest of the morning and early afternoon talking about the wedding plans while I sneak in texts to my managers to check on the resort. So far there are no problems, but no one has seen my receptionist. I informed them that she hasn't called in and that maybe someone should check her place, but I had no plans of leaving my home after nearly being killed.

11

Maria

I'M STANDING in the middle of the station's bullpen with two dozen officers, some on duty, others here just for the meeting. "Hello, everyone. Some of you may already know me as Mr. Turner's fiancée, but before that I was a Deputy for the Wolfe Creek Police Department for several years. I'm filling in as an interim chief of police. As you are aware, when the former chief learned of his impending firing, he attacked Aria Turner, who protected me, and then Mr. Turner the following morning after faking his death. His fate was of his own making. Now, I know I'm a woman and new to the area, but I'm not the kind to ruffle feathers. If you have a problem with me, you better figure it out, or move on to another position. We will not have another Anderson incident. This town has been limited to one murder a year for decades, and we will attempt to keep it that way or even better from now on. I am sorry that things ended up this way for Anderson. Do any of you have any questions?"

"Yes—do you have a sister?"

"No, she doesn't," Turner snarls out from the back of the room.

"But I have lots of cousins. In all seriousness, it's going to take a little bit for me to get accustomed to the setup here, and I might make some changes. For the time being, the schedules will stay the same. If you have any questions, please don't hesitate." I shake hands with each and every one of them before heading into Anderson's former office. The chair has been changed and the desk cleared out and examined by the forensic team.

"Hello, I'm Agnes, one of the four dispatchers here. I just thought I'd introduce myself. My mate is one of Turner's cousins and Officer Holden out there. The one who's talking to Turner right now." I look through the large glass window with the blinds turned open.

I smile and think to myself how much they look alike. Not identical in any way, but the family resemblance is there. "It's a pleasure to meet you."

"I'm not sure if you know this, but I'm with pups, and, well, I'm going to be taking time off in a couple of months to birth them, but I can't say that I'll be returning. My mate isn't happy with everything that's going on and is too worried about me."

"I understand. I hope we don't have any more crazy people living with pent-up jealousy."

"I hope not either, but we don't really need the money. I'd been working here before we mated, so it's not like I just up and quit, but our relationship caught

Anderson's notice a little more than I expected it to. There's no policy against it since, well, you know."

"Yes, I know. Well, let me know when you have to leave. Are you having a baby shower or anything?"

"Yes. My mom is throwing one next week. You're welcome to come, of course."

"You don't have to invite me as your boss."

"It's not because you're my boss. You're the Alpha's mate and one we all will defer to, so it would be wonderful to have you there. You don't have to bring anything, but I would love for you to meet some of the other females in the pack." I ask her for the info and enter it into the calendar on my phone. I want to get to know the women. Turner did inform me that I will be the one female shifters will come to with questions or concerns, as well as someone to admire.

"Thank you. Well, I better get going. I have to start my shift." She smiles and walks out. I'm so glad I don't have to worry about the females on the force. Every single female is a shifter. It makes my life easier.

A light knock on my door brings a smile to my face. "What can I do for you, Mr. Turner?"

"I can think of many things, but I have to head out. I wanted to see you one more time before I go."

"I'm going to be okay. If it makes you feel better, I could have one of them stand at my door and protect me."

"I would feel better. That's a great idea. Holden will do it." He kisses me hard and walks out, and then Holden approaches and without a word, stands outside my door. I laugh and shake my head.

One by one, a few officers come in and say hello. I don't get cold glares or anything from them, and the day goes about as normal as it can. The one officer that could be promoted to sheriff is a shifter, and he knows that the Alpha's edict is golden, so he doesn't pitch a fit.

"It's about seven at night and quitting time for me. Does anyone need anything from me?"

"No thanks, Chief. Congrats on your first day," Officer Peck says.

A round of applause fills the station. I'd gone on patrol to get a sense of the area and then I de-escalated two situations with some guests, one fender-bender and another at the bar. It had been a remarkably busy and interesting day. Now, I want to go home and snuggle with Turner for a bit.

I shut down everything in my office and lock the door before lifting my gaze to see Turner waiting for me. A smile washes over my face, but I maintain my cool and walk up to him with the dignity of the chief of police.

"Are you ready, Chief?"

"Yes, Mr. Turner." I'm smiling all the way to his vehicle because even though I'm tired, I'm glad to be with my mate.

He leads me out to his SUV and we climb inside, and then we head back to the house. We are both exhausted, but I need him. Reading me as always, his mouth is on mine. We barely make it in the house when he tears off my clothes and frees himself. With one thrust, he's buried inside me on the foyer floor on all fours. We growl and moan as he pounds into me, gripping my shoulders and dominating my body. Our bodies rock and shake as he drills me hard.

"Come for me, Maria."

"Yes, Alpha," I cry out, squeezing his cock as my pussy pulsates and my soul comes apart. He roars, biting down on my neck as he fills me up. We collapse on the floor and rest.

"Do you think we could do that as wolves?"

"We can, if you want," he growls against my ear. "I'd love to feel your fur against mine as we fuck."

Heat fills my core just thinking about us together. "Let me rest a bit, and then you can take me hard in the middle of the forest under the moonlight."

"Let me take you to bed." We both stand, and then he picks me up in his arms and carries me to our room. Life is so good.

We wake up just after midnight, and the moon is high. "How about a run?"

"Ooh, that sounds good." It's perfect. I rush out of bed and run downstairs. He follows after me and catches me before we get to the door. "Put some clothes on. We'll shift where no one can see us."

"Oh goodness. I didn't think of that."

"There's no one around, but I don't want anyone to steal a glance at you naked, even at a distance. I'm fucking jealous."

We put on some clothes and then he leads me into a thicket. "Strip, baby."

"Yes, Alpha." I quickly remove my clothes and watch Turner do the same. Suddenly he shifts, and he's so beautiful. I relax and let my body shift.

He howls and growls. *You're so sexy, my mate.*

You're majestic, my Alpha.

Let's run, and then I'm going to drill your little slit until we pass out.

We dash through the snow, and it's so fun. I never expected to do something wild like this. By the time we stop, we're atop a hill looking down. Strangely, I'm not afraid, turning to smile at Turner, and then I take off down the slope. I race to the bottom, but he's so much larger and faster that he passes me by and beats me to the bottom. Turner's back paws swing around, bringing himself to a stop and staring directly at me. His eyes darken and become intense.

Get over here.

I dip my head and run it along his throat. *I love you.*

He mounts me from behind, and we fuck like wild animals. It's different and exciting, but it doesn't beat the feel of our human forms gliding together. We both howl our release and then rest until we can catch our breath. We shift, he carries me into the thicket, and he helps me dress.

"Damn, Maria. You are sexy either way. I love being inside you any way I can, whether it's on all fours covered in fur, or you on my desk with your thighs wrapped around me."

"I'll take it all, Turner."

12

Turner

I STAND face to face with Maria's father. I shouldn't be intimidated, but he's the man who gave me her. He doesn't even understand the significance of this day. It's just tying her in the human way, but we're connected in so many more ways. Her mother looked at her stomach the second she arrived, and yes, my mate is going to have our first pup, and it was hard to hide. She wasn't showing, but her waist had thickened.

"Hello, Senor Arroyo. I'm so glad that you could make it. Maria said there was a terrible storm that caused damage to the area."

"Yes, but we were able to board everything up and make our way on time. Thank you for leaving the plane for us. I wouldn't want to miss this for anything in the world."

"I would have postponed it," I state while I adjust my cuffs.

"You have over two hundred guests here."

"Maria's happiness is of the utmost importance to me. It's a good thing we're doing this in the main resort, though."

"I'm surprised—for as much money you have, you live in a simple, but modern large cabin."

"Unless we're having a dozen children, I don't see the need for something more."

"Ah, son. There you are," my father says, coming up to us.

"Hello, I'm Mayor Marcus Turner. You must be the father of the bride I've heard so much about."

"Mayor?"

"Yes, it's ceremonial, really. This place runs smoothly, especially with our new chief of police. Maria has been fantastic."

"Maria's the chief of police? She didn't tell us that."

"Yes, well, she's only going to stay in the position temporarily and doesn't want anyone to get used to it."

"That's still incredible. Why only temporary?" His hackles are raised, but I don't blame the man because she's his little girl and he wants her happiness.

"Because she's pregnant, Antonio," Maria's mother says, coming up to me with a grin.

"What?" That doesn't calm him down for the exact same reason. I knocked up his baby girl.

"Well, that's another reason, but as you can see, it's not something I'd go through all the trouble to hide. We only found out two days ago, as it happens, and she's not far along at all." It's the truth, although she may not be pregnant for the full nine months—but it will be close. According to what I learned from Hunter, it can be anywhere from seven to nine months, and they'll still be healthy. The baby and mother determine how fast it happens, but that's all we know.

"That's what she said, but that means you two rushed this. Are you sure you're not going to have second thoughts?"

"I'm positive as can be."

"Are you sure she is, though?" Now he's trying to push my buttons, but it won't work one bit. I pretend to be off in space, pondering his question.

Babe, are you sure you want to marry me?

Of course—why would you ask that?

Your parents are asking me if I'm sure.

You better be. You can't unmark me.

I don't want to.

"I'm sure she doesn't. Please enjoy your time. The wedding will be starting soon. You don't want to miss your time with Maria before I whisk her away." I look over, and there's Jacob standing next to the door where Aria's getting ready. I walk over to him and grab him by the shoulder. "Remember there are plenty of humans here. Get your ass under control. I know my sister's going to look beautiful."

"I know," he mutters, glaring at every male in the room. I can't say I blame the poor bastard.

"They can't have her," I remind him, which does calm him slightly.

"I know." Jacob tugs on his collar, feeling like he's suffocating, and I understand his energy because I'm nearly as bad as him, but I know that no one can take my woman away from me.

"You're still jealous."

"You know."

"I do. Take it easy, and remember—it's only another ten months."

"It's more like eleven."

"I was trying to help you out. Stand strong. I'm letting you walk her down the aisle for a reason. You better behave."

"I will. I promise." I owe him, even if I don't want to admit it. If it wasn't for his actions, I wouldn't have met my mate. I can't even fathom the agony of not knowing her.

"It's your turn to behave, Alpha," he whispers. "Your eyes. She's here, and yours."

"I don't know if that emotion will ever get better. I long for her and need her, and there's not a single thing that can stop that feeling. I know you understand."

"That I do. Thank you."

"It's time," Max says. "Last chance to run." I arch my brow, and he smiles like the asshole he is. He's going to school much closer to home but still has the same feelings towards mating. Although he's happy to be out of the heat, he's instead attending the University of Oregon.

"To the altar. That's the only place I'm running right now."

"Fine. I'm just saying." He nudges me, and then I walk up the aisle.

Max is my best man, and Daphne is Maria's Matron of Honor. She managed to put the wedding together easily while nursing a newborn, and so far there isn't a thing that's not been perfect.

I stand there, waiting for my bride to come to me. My heart races as the music begins. I'm not worried, nor do I have cold feet like a traditional groom. She's already mine. I've already made sure of that. Our bond is greater than a piece of paper. This is a soul contract. Her wolf and my wolf are one for the rest of our days. Still, as the doors open, the smile on my face can't seem to go down. Luckily, I adjusted my cock to rest under my belt, and my tux jacket covers it or I'd give everyone a show.

The bridesmaids and groomsmen make their way to the front, but all I wait for is my queen. She comes out, and I'm floored. Her full-length ball gown is truly the gown of a queen. It even has a grand cape that trails behind her as the long sleeves rest off her shoulders, displaying her delectable collarbone. I'm glad her bite marks fade to the naked human eye. Everyone stands as she makes her way down the aisle on her father's arm looking like absolute perfection. Her long black hair is pinned up in a super elegant updo that I'm going to tear apart by the end of the night, but I promised to let her get through the pictures at least.

Her eyes meet mine, and I lose it. I'm nearly on my way to grab her when Max grips my arm. "She's almost to you. Let the man have his joy."

Be patient. I'm coming, Alpha.

You'll be repeating that tonight. Over and over again.

She nearly stumbles and then narrows her eyes at me while still maintaining her smile for the guests and the cameras.

Pussy tingling?

Asshole.

That too? I'll take you any way you want. Maybe on all fours after a long run.

Her wolf and mine have been out playing over and over every other night before coming home and making love in front of the fire.

"Who gives this woman to this man?" Both of us are stunned, realizing that we'd been too focused on later to hear the priest.

"I do." Senor Arroyo kisses his daughter's cheek and then places her hand in mine. "Take care of my girl."

"Forever." He nods and takes his seat.

The ceremony passes in a blur as I stare at my other half, the best part of myself. She's everything and so much more. I pull her into my arms for our kiss. I do my best to make it as chaste as possible because I've already had glares from every man in her family. They can respect the fact that I'm wealthy, so knocking her up isn't so bad, especially because I was anxious to get married. My people gather around, cheering us and bowing slightly. We have nearly half the shifters in the area who aren't working in attendance.

Erik and his wife, Chloe, come up to us as we enter the grand reception area. "Congratulations. I'm sorry Hunter and Cat couldn't make it." I understand more than anyone how busy a hotel can be, plus they have a family, which means less time and a lot more chaos.

"He called me this morning. An overflowing tub in a suite, and Cat's sick."

"Yep. Another little one on the way."

"I appreciate you two coming out to make it."

"Cat would have loved to have gotten away from the kids tonight, but since she's knocked up and they were available, we left our kids with them," Chloe says, hugging Maria.

"We're glad to have you."

"When do we eat, because I can't wait to twirl my wife around the floor."

"Me too, me too." We excuse ourselves and go around the room greeting our guests. It turns out to be an amazing night, but all I want to do is be in bed with my love. At about ten, we call it a night and thank all of our guests. Her family is staying at the hotel, and we'll be back for lunch with them tomorrow, but for now, I need to hold Maria and make slow, lazy love to her.

We hurry and exit before they can stop us. The drive is short, so we're home in a flash. I carry her over the threshold and then lock the door behind me as I rush up to our bedroom. I have her naked in less than two minutes, and it takes another two to get me completely naked. "Fuck, you're sexy as hell, wife."

"Make love to me, my husband." And I do. Slow, deep, and with love until we're both sleeping in a sweaty passionate mess.

EPILOGUE

Maria

"GET BACK HERE," I call out, running after my five-year-old son who's bolting out the front door and shifting. He's going to be in big trouble when Daddy comes home, and like clockwork, Turner pulls into the driveway. Marcus comes to a halt and he pads back and forth, waiting for Daddy. He couldn't wait to show his daddy what he learned, but someone could have seen him.

"Marcus, wow! You did it!" Marcus's tail wags wildly, full of pride. The boy is a handful. Turner looks up at me and lets out a growl.

Your blouse is unbuttoned.

I look down and say, "Oh shit." I was feeding the little one when someone took off.

"Marcus, come inside now." A whimpering whine comes from my little wolf, but he's going to have to learn some new things. The second Marcus is through the door, Turner says, "Change back." He does, and I give him a towel that I just folded to wrap around himself.

"Come over here," Turner orders calmly, but his little replica does it with his chin down. "Don't duck your head. First, I'm proud of you that you shifted on your own, but...do you know why I'm upset?"

"Because I didn't listen to Mommy."

"Yes. See, she's my queen, and anything that upsets Mommy upsets me."

"I thought Mommy would be happy," he cries.

"She would be if you waited for her to finish feeding the baby and for her to make sure no humans were around. If you had shifted and a human saw you, we'd have a big problem. You know that, right?"

"Yes," he sighs, knowing we're disappointed with his behavior.

"Next time, you and I can go together."

"Really?"

"Yes. Give Daddy a few minutes with Mommy." I watch the way my husband's eyes stare at my breasts. I can feel his need, hunger running through him.

"How's the baby?"

"Asleep."

"Well fed?"

"Yes, Alpha."

He reaches out and checks the front locks without taking his eyes off of me. "Go put your clothes on and then go into your playroom, son."

"Okay, Daddy."

"Good boy." He runs up the stairs while my man stares at me, licking his lips.

"Did you need something, Alpha?"

"You showed my tits to the world."

"No one was out there. I had to run after your son."

"I know, which is the only reason I'm calm. Now, in the kitchen right now." I follow his instructions and head into the kitchen where I've just finished making a French silk pie for dessert. I have on a light material dress that has buttons running down the top part, freeing my breasts easily so I can feed the little one. He's five months old, and now I'm already pregnant for a third time, but I'm trying to keep it a secret from Turner.

You have no secrets, mate. I scent our next little one in your womb.

He turns his attention to the pie, and then I find myself planted on the counter. His fingers skim up my legs until he reaches the hem of my panties and hooks them around the material, tugging them down my thighs. "These have to go." He drops them on the floor. "You're mine, Maria. You know I'd have to rip anyone's eyes out if they saw your tits."

"I'm sorry, Alpha."

"Oh, that's not going to cut it. I need to show you how much you mean to me. How insane I am and how much I need you." He scissors his fingers in my folds. "Fuck, you feel like you really need me."

"I do, Turner." He shakes his head and raises his brow, stopping the teasing of my slit. "Alpha."

"Good girl." Bringing his fingers to his lips, he sucks my juices off. "Hmm...I put another little one inside you. Good. Very good. What do you need, Maria?" I need what he needs. Our needs match, and he knows it. I give him a slight shove and then drop to my knees as he unbuckles his slacks. I help, sliding his zipper down and then yanking his waistband down, freeing his thick cock. My fingers wrap around the length as I slip the head past my lips. "Fuck, Maria."

"Yes, Alpha," I moan. I'm so horny that I'm close to coming right now. My pussy throbs so much that I'm strumming it with my other hand. Turner takes over, gathering my hair into his fist and fucking my face. I gag and then relax as he pulls back out. We repeat it, picking up the pace as he stuffs his long, thick rod down my throat. The cold metal of his wedding ring rests on my cheek as he cups my face, using my mouth. I cry out around his shaft, coming hard. He pulls out, and then I'm spread out on the counter. With his quick hands he stops the pie from falling, but then he swipes his tongue along my seam and I suddenly forget all about the pie. My hands are over my head, grasping onto the edge of the counter while my mate devours my still spasming cunt. I'll never get enough of watching his eyes glow as his wolf is ready to spring forward. "Alpha. I'm coming."

Good. Coat my face before I coat your pussy. I've got a load that's been waiting for your heat all damn day.

His words rip through me and I cry out, coming on his tongue. I slap my hand over my mouth to muffle the sound. Chuckling with a deep rumble, he pulls me to the edge and slams deep inside, sending me closer to another orgasm. Gripping the top of my dress and my bra, he uses it as a handle as he drills me hard. "Come again. Cover that pretty mouth of yours and then come on my cock so I can let go." His other hand goes around my throat, massaging it as he beats my pussy up. I shut my mouth tight and hold back the scream.

Ahhh. I'm coming, Alpha. Give me your seed. Yes. Yes. Yes. Fuck me.

Turner roars and fills me up, collapsing on me, his head pressed on my chest as he catches his breath.

"I was kidding. Earlier. No one saw your tits because I didn't even see them. I just couldn't help myself."

"Well, then, I'll make sure a couple of buttons are undone tomorrow."

"We're going to need a babysitter for that."

"Taken care of, Alpha."

"God, I love you, Maria."

---

*L*ater at dinner, we're gathered at the table with his parents, and little Marcus tells them about his shifting. "But I got Mommy in trouble and I could hear Daddy spanking Mommy in the kitchen. I'm sorry, Mommy. I'll behave." I don't think there's a name for the shade of red I turned. Even Turner had no response immediately for it.

It's Grandpa Turner who says, "It's okay, baby boy. I'm sure Mommy didn't learn her lesson at all, but now you know to listen to your mother." He winks at Turner, who's doing his best not to laugh.

"Sorry, buddy. Mommy and I were only play wrestling. I wouldn't hurt your mom even when she's a bad girl. You, though—you'll get a spanking if you run out like that again."

"Okay, Daddy." He then goes on to tell them the sprinting he and Daddy went on while I cleaned the kitchen and cooked dinner. They were two handsome men. I look at the baby boy in the cradle next to the table, and he looks just like his daddy as well.

We still have to work on his discretion. I'm glad you wanted him isolated from the human students.

I nod and feel Turner's hand grip my thigh. *I love you, Maria. Next time, though, I'll have to be careful to cover your mouth.*

Maybe the kitchen's a bad idea.

Maybe the kid needs some headphones.

A much better idea.

THE END

Find more about C.M. Steele on:

Website/Newsletter: www.cmsteele.com
Amazon Author Page: www.amazon.com/C-M-
Steele/e/B00MQ9FPZS/
Facebook: www.facebook.com/CMsteele2014
FB Reader Group: https://www.facebook.com/
groups/1190691734281008/
Instagram: https://www.instagram.com/c.m._steele/
Twitter: https://twitter.com/Author_CMSteele
Bookbub: https://www.bookbub.com/authors/c-m-steele

EXPCERPT FROM WOLFE'S DEN:

Hunter

"Any news on the woman fitting my description?" I asked my sister as she sat in my office. We had other matters to discuss, but my entire being focused on the other half of my existence that was physically missing. The past six months had been unbearable torture. I hungered for my mate and yet, I had no idea who she was or how I would find her. Her sexy curves and curly brown hair tormented my every waking hour.

Chloe fidgeted in her seat, and I knew there had been no progress. It was hard on her to watch me slowly lose my mind. I shifted every night, running for hours, trying to fight sleep because dreaming of her was too much, but staying away from her was just as hard. With my body and soul exhausted, I took it out on my people.

"Sorry, Hunter. We can't seem to locate her in any of the packs in the Northwest. Gage is about to go down to the southwest territories and see if any female meets your description." A weary expression formed on her normally stoic face. I depended on Chloe when it came to a lot of the operational details of the resort, and I knew I was putting too much on her, but I didn't trust anyone else aside from her or my brother, Gage, to help me find this woman. Unfortunately my second in command couldn't be trusted either with so big a task that could be my greatest strength or my complete ruin.

"I need to find her. These dreams are slowly killing me. She's my mate. I need to find her," I snarled. Every day I struggled to contain my wolf. He wanted to leave the area in search of her, but being the Alpha, I had to remain strong and do what I had to do for the rest of the pack, which required bringing in more revenue by opening the resort.

My emotions were coming to a head, to the point of nearly giving away to the beast inside. I had to shave twice a day because my wolf laid at the surface of my soul. No matter how much I tried to calm the beast, he came to life after he claimed her each night. I was a shaggy mess every morning, and this morning was no different. My eyes, body and soul were exhausted, but I had to carry on for my people.

I needed to focus on the resort, but I wanted answers on my mysterious mate.

Chloe's green eyes dilated, and a sense of foreboding came over her as she nervously asked, "Hunter...what if she's not in a pack? What if she's a human?" The thought had crossed my mind if only for a brief moment since it was impossible for us to mate with one.

"There's never been a female human in our pack.

Have you ever heard any tales about it?" Regretfully, I hadn't heard anything about such a thing, but at this point, I wouldn't care. As a Northwest American clan, we weren't as informed about our past as we would have liked to have been. In the late 1740s, a massive brush fire ripped through our lands burning every in its path, including most of our historical records. The surviving members of the packs moved further north settle along the Cascade Mountains. The remaining records were kept secure with pack historians for safekeeping.

Rumors spread that the great fire had been set intentionally by one of our own in an attempt to end the lives of the Alpha's family, *my family*, and destroy our pack history so that they could create a new one.

"No, but we can call the elder in Redding to see if he has any idea if it's even possible," Chloe suggested. She did have a point. Creed and his family had some old books, none of which were very detailed or if they were, they had been singed too severely to even be interpreted.

Gossip about our past floated through our village just like any other. There were claims that there was a human mate, but it was just a myth to give some of the pack hope when a member took too long to find their mate. But with all the searching for my mate and no luck, I was starting to believe in that tale.

"I need to find her. She's mine. I'm thirty-two already. I should have found my mate many years ago," I growled, the pain of never finding her ripping through my chest. Erotic dreams weren't a thing for our species. Once our mate was found, we smelled each other and mated within the day. I'd been dreaming of her for six months, reliving night after night of overwhelming, heart-pounding passion that defied belief. Maybe it was no different for other shifters in that area, not that I would know or would ask, but I felt her soul as we mated in my sleep.

"We'll find her," she promised. The determination and conviction in her voice made me believe her. Brushing off her skirt and laying her tablet on my desk, she said, "Let's try to take your mind off the mating hunger and talk shop."

I sighed. "That's probably for the best." She was right, as always. I wished I could have made her my Beta, but unfortunately it was passed down from generation to generation from another pack family. It was our own way of checks and balances. One family couldn't possess total control.

"We only have a month before we open, and we haven't even started the hiring process. I know there are several locals that need jobs, but we need more than them," she remarked. I knew where she was going with this, but I was too riled up with mating hunger that I ignored it. She'd been pestering me for weeks about hiring not only shifters but humans as well.

"I'd say in the next two weeks, we can start hiring the local community to run the resort," I added.

Immediately her eyes opened wide and she snapped her fingers, a little quirk of hers when she had a brilliant idea or remembered something. "Oh, yes, we've already received a call about a job from a woman in Oregon named Catherine. She sounded desperate. I feel terrible that we can't hire her." Chloe was truly soft at heart unless you fucked with her family. It was in her personality to care about a kitten, something laughable to our kind.

"Is she a shifter?" I asked, knowing that was probably not the case because Chloe had the power to hire shifters without permission A human on the other hand would be a bad idea.

"No, she's a human, but she sounds like she's about to break if we don't hire her. Gage thinks we should. It would help if we hired a few humans." I gave her the warning glare. We talked about this before and I wasn't totally against it, but I wanted to be super selective if we did hire one of them. And pity wasn't a reason to hire a human. It's one thing to see them in passing as guests, but daily contact could risk everything for our kind. "Don't look at me like that. I know the danger of daily interaction with the same people, but just...well, just listen to her message." Chloe got up and leaned over my desk, then dialed the number for the company mailbox and her voicemail access code and put it on speaker.

"Um. Hello, this is Catherine Kinney...I know you didn't have an application for employment up, but I really need a job..." she sighed. I hit the replay button, not letting her message finish. Chloe looked at me in disbelief. I didn't answer her stare. I listened to the same part again. My body coursing with electricity as a cascade of emotions flowed over me as I listen her desperate message.

A growl ripped through my chest and I demanded, "Bring her to me."

I continued to listen to the plea from the warm voice I'd come to worship. I knew every inch of her body, the beat of her heart, the taste of her flesh, and the scent that drove the beast in me insane with hunger. Most of all, I knew what it was like to hear her sighs of ecstasy as I claimed her every night. It was *her*. My mate.

"Hunter, are you well?" Chloe asked as she sat straight up. I was feeling a range of emotions, and it was noticeable in my eyes and the sudden release of my fangs, rattling my sister who was concerned for me. *Catherine.* She was real, she was mine, and I wasn't going to let anything stop me from claiming her.

"It's *her*. Get her to take the job," I snarled. I stood up and paced the room, my blood pumping through my body, forcing the other me to come to the surface. I could feel the shift coming, but I fought it back.

"Wait—*her*? As in your mate?" she asked as she turned in her seat to look at me with a confused expression. I could only snarl at the stupid question.

"Find a picture of her. Now!" I roared as I continued to pace with building tension.

ABOUT THE AUTHOR

C.M. Steele is a bestselling author on Amazon with over 100 books to read and enjoy!

C.M. Steele's Book List:

Best Friends Series:

Always You

His Dirty Secret

Sleep Tight

A Best Friends Duet:

Picture Perfect

Instant Obsession

The Captive Series:

Luciano's Willing Captive

The Russian's Captive

Sergei's Stubborn Captive

The Caught Series:

Caught In A Case

Caught Off Guard

Caught in A Lie

Caught Crossing the Line

Caught Breaking the Law

Caught Red Handed

Cavanaugh Security Series:

Protecting Macy

Securing Blake

The Lamian Wars:

Bound

Reveal

Release

All Hallows Eve

Love Bites Series:

Love Bites

Once Bitten

The Middleton Hotels:

Built for Me

Built to Last

Built Strong

Built Over Time

Built Overnight

Nothing but Trouble Series:

Taking the Bait

Taking the Mafia Princess

The O'Connell Family:

Claiming Red

Burning for Claire

Claiming Abby

Reminding Red

Obsessed Alpha Series:

Stone

Cole

Graham

Theo

Maddox

Alessandro

A Rough Hands Novella:

My Miracle

Nailing my Wife

Say Something Series:

Say Uncle

Say Please

Say Uncle: Doggy Style

Sister Switch:

Testing Her Professor

Assisting Her Boss

Special Forces: Operation Alpha (Susan Stoker's World):

Guarding Hope

Guarding Forever

A Steele Christmas:

Mason's Winter

Perfectly Wrapped

The Company You Keep

A Steele Fairy Tale:

My Gold

My Forever

My Property

My Prince Charming

A Steele Riders Family Novella Series:

Holiday Knockout

His Siren

A Steele Riders MC Series:

Boomer

Mick

Jackson

Doc

Beast

Ghost

Wrench

Southern Hospitality:

Down South

Gone South

Sweetheart's Treats:

Sweet Surprise

Doctor's Orders, Sweetheart

Sweet Surrender

Twin Sin:

Stalk Me Please

Sinful Intent

White Wolf Ridge Series:

Turner

Wolfe Creek Series:

Wolfe's Den

Beta: Her Alpha

Raging Kane

Written in History

Others:

Buying Love

Christmas in Camden

Conquering Alexandria

Grant's Deal

Hunting Allegra

Killer Abs

Love Discovered

Loving My Neighbor

Mrs. Valentine

My Christmas Gift

Rainy Days Stormy Nights

Red Hot Nights
Scarred
Sharp Curves
So Wrong
Standing There
Stealing Beauty
Taking the Thief
The Wedding Guest
Unexpected